CW00765048

WELSH HEIRS

Welsh Heirs

GLYN JONES

GOMER PRESS

1977

First Impression—November 1977

ISBN 0 85088 495 0

© THE AUTHOR AND GOMER PRESS

*This volume is published with the support
of the Welsh Arts Council*

PRINTED BY J. D. LEWIS AND SONS LTD.
GOMER PRESS, LLANDYSUL

CONTENTS

ROBERT JEFFREYS

When I first came to live in the Ystrad valley I was bewildered by the number and the variety of the shocks to which the assumptions of my upbringing had made me subject. But in one matter I was extremely fortunate. My first landlord was a Mr. Robert Jeffreys, a voluble ex-collier, eloquent in two languages. He spoke English copiously, but in his sustained story-telling he used Welsh, so it seemed to me, like a poet, like those uninhibited natures we read of whose work flows, who produce poems as naturally, as abundantly, and as effortlessly as a great tree puts out its foliage. He lived with his wife and his unmarried son, Gareth, in Morlais Road, a pleasant street not far from St. Teilo's church where I served as curate. There was another child, a married daughter, Myra Powell, who, with her husband and two children, occupied a house on the hillside overlooking the town, a house Mr. and Mrs. Jeffreys had themselves once lived in, early in their marriage.

Mr. Herbert, Mr. Jeffreys said to me at one of our early meetings, wagging before my face his mutilated index with a thick bunch of black hairs sprouting like a little brush out of the first knuckle, where it ended—Mr. Herbert, you leave it to me. I am the Bobby Greencoat in these parts and I know it all. My job takes me everywhere. I see everything. You don't know what a Bobby Greencoat is ? Well, I am the Whipper-in. No? The school attendance officer then, and if the children are absent, or late, or miching, I am the one to hunt them up and summonse them. If you want to know anything about this valley, Mr. Herbert, you leave it to me. I have heard who is expecting sooner than the midwife and who stole the chickens long before the sergeant. Talking about chickens, I was in one of those cottages—they're more like ruins—down there by the canal side this afternoon looking for a micher—a rum lot they are down there I can tell you—and do you know what they were up to ? They had stretched wire netting round the legs of the kitchen table and they were trying to raise a brood of Buff Orpingtons under it. Now what do you think of that ? You leave it to me, Mr. Herbert, because I see it all.

A stocky man, he grinned up at me, his spectacles twinkling and the pair of eff-shaped cello-marks deepening on his swarthy cheeks.

After completing my course at the theological college I came to this mining valley curacy from mixed proselitizing zeal and a kind of romantic or sentimental interest in, to me, so enigmatical a region. My father, although most of his life had been spent in incumbencies in the more genteel parishes of outer London, was a native of North Wales. In consequence the languages of the various English vicarages in which I was brought up were Welsh and German—German because my mother came from Heidelberg where my father had been a student at the university. I found many of the characteristics of the valley therefore, the universal dissent, the pervading egalitarianism, the powerful sense of community and of clan, at first strange and disturbing in their intensity. For one of our poorer parishoners, I remember, a young Mrs. Richards, I secured a regular supply of paid sewing from a patroness of my father devoted to charitable works. Mrs. Richards received a large roll of towel-cloth every month which she undertook to make up into diapers for use in some orphanage Lady Harriet was interested in. But after a while I found that Mrs. Richards was not returning all the articles she had cut out and stitched, and that several of her neighbours were benefitting by this dereliction. I was angry, but when I remonstrated with her she treated the matter coolly and laughed. "Don't you worry about it, Mr. Herbert," she said cheerfully, "*God understands me.*"

I was completely baffled by this reply and when I returned to my lodgings I mentioned to Mr. Jeffreys what had happened. He heard me with nodded understanding, but proved to me, with more theology than I could then counter, that her attitude was really unexceptionable, that she was benefitting herself not at all, that she was giving up her time to sewing for her poorer neighbours, that the diapers were in any case intended for the needy, and so on and so on, the sophisms delivered in a torrent of unanswerable Welsh eloquence. I realized then I had to deal with a race of strange and powerful loyalties, of dangerous persuasiveness in the justification of alien modes of thought and feeling.

It was my habit from the beginning to take a stroll every night after supper a little way along the road which lead up the side of the mountain and eventually over into the next valley, and sometimes on my walk Mr. Jeffreys came with me. One night, as we were setting out in the dark, rather later than usual, through the deserted streets of Ystrad, an event occurred which for me dispelled forever the easy assumptions of my youth and upbringing and brought me nearer than I had ever been before to the life lived in those strange and perplexing valleys.

Although it was fine when we set out, the rain had been falling previously and had put a gleam over the dark wet streets like the sheen of steel in the lamplight. No one was about at that time of night and Mr. Jeffreys' theology was for long periods uninterrupted by acknowledgement or greeting. But as we were approaching the circle of brightness under one of the gas-lamps of the empty street I noticed the large uncertain figure of a man approaching us from the far side of the light, his clothes taking on the greenish brightness as he swayed forward out of the dark toward us. He was tall, wearing a bowler hat and a dark baggy overcoat that seemed to bang about his person as he came rocking forward. His advance into the light was crooked and prowling and I supposed at first that he must be drunk. But an observable regularity, an ordered rhythm in his uncertainty, suggested that some physical infirmity, rather, was perhaps the cause of this pitiful and ungainly shamble. We met directly under the street lamp and Mr. Jeffreys gave up his lengthy footnote abruptly to speak to him.

"Dafydd," he said in Welsh. "How are you ? I haven't seen you a long time. Where have you been keeping yourself ?"

The trance-like expression on the old man's face was replaced by a quick glance of apprehension. But as Mr. Jeffreys tumbled out questions and information he became calm again, he took off his hat and seemed to brood over us in silence, a look of profound sadness and humility upon his face.

And, as he stood in the clear gaslight, I studied him with some inexplicable fascination. He was a tall man but he stooped forward so that his shoulders were rounded and his chest hollowed. His head was large and beautiful, it seemed like heavy ivory become mellowed and yellowish, it was ponderous and comely, the eyes greatly overhung, the nose slender and delicate, the silvery hair thick and stiff and brushed forward carelessly in a fringe over the brow. The flesh of the cleanshaven face was everywhere firm and grooved ; across the flat forehead, sloping outwards to the thick brows, rows of deep lines were immovably scored, each incision clean-cut and furrow-shaped ; a bunch of wrinkles converged upon the outer corners of his eyes ; fine grooves were present along the flanks of his nose ; and upon his hollow cheeks one oblique and intricate meshwork seemed superimposed at an angle upon an earlier pattern, as though the sufferings of two different lives were recorded in that elaborate interweaving. The body beneath the massive head was proportionately bulky but as he stood listening to the talk it seemed shapeless, negligible, an appendage almost to the magnificence of the sorrowful features.

The old man was wearing a clumsy black overcoat, long, and reaching up to his throat, the buttons lost or dangling loose through the gaping buttonholes, the elbows patched with tweed. The bowler had lost its rigidity and seemed soft as a cloth hat in his fingers.

The one-sided conversation proceeded for a while and then abruptly it was all over. At the sound of working boots approaching along the pavement the old man glanced round anxiously and put on his hat. "I must be going. Good-night, sir," he said to me in his deep gentle voice. Then he turned to Mr. Jeffreys and took his hand. "Good-night, Robert," he said. "Good-night. And God bless you for talking to me." With that he lurched off into the darkness, his patched overcoat knocking against him as he went.

I felt strangely involved in this meeting although I had scarcely uttered a word during its brief duration. And I wished very much to learn more about the handsome and shabby old man whose blessing followed the simple act of speaking to him.

Poor Dafydd, Mr. Jeffreys said, looking back after him. There he goes again. Up to Bethesda, I feel sure of it. Let's watch him, indeed, Mr. Herbert. If we walk back a few yards we can see what he will be doing.

Protesting, but not entirely unwilling, I went. From the corner of the next side street we could see the old man standing at the open door of one of the houses half-way along it with the light from the passage painted upon him. The by-street itself was deserted and unlighted. In a moment or two, as we watched, a little girl appeared on the doorstep and handed something out to him. Then the front door shut and the old man shambled away down the street into the darkness.

There you are, said Mr. Jeffreys. Did you see that ? Thomas the Bethesda caretaker lives in that house. I thought it was the chapel key he was after. Dafydd can't leave the place alone. Every Wednesday night he's there, they say, sitting by himself in the gallery and the whole place in darkness. Some say he will rise and conduct an imaginary congregation, or the singing of an absent choir in an anthem or a chorus, but that is something I do not readily believe about him. Poor Dafydd.

Let me tell you then, he went on, answering me. He is Dafydd Morris and he used to be a grocer in the valley here. At one time he kept the *Crown Stores*, that old-fashioned little place in Station Street, opposite the wall of the railway embankment. You know it. With the covered lane along-side and the bakehouse out at the back.

I remembered the little shop, it was low and dark, I had seen many like it in the valley since my arrival. There was a large yellow crown painted on the wall between the windows of what seemed to be the living quarters upstairs. To get into the shop from the pavement one went down three or four stone steps. The floor was always covered with sawdust, and the gaslights were often on even in the daytime. When you passed the doorway, especially in hot weather, you noticed a very powerful smell of floor polish and lard.

I remembered these things as Mr. Jeffreys described for me Dafydd Morris conducting, Dafydd Morris singing, Dafydd

13

Morris working underground, all in his torrential Welsh ; climbing the mountain road in the darkness he recalled vividly what he had seen, heard and imagined of the old man's life, all that had led up to the knocking at the door in the side street and the handing out of the chapel key.

Dafydd Morris bought the stock and goodwill of the *Crown Stores*, and the bakery behind it, he told me, partly with the money collected for him by us, his fellow colliers, when it became clear his accident would make him say goodbye to the pit for ever. But he was always an indifferent man of business. I remember his telling me once that when he was out on his rounds delivering bread he would never *at the time* enter in his book how many loaves each customer had bought, he would rely on his memory and do it all when he got back to the shop at night. I have often seen him driving his bread cart up along this road we are on now. And on the cliff up there, Mr. Herbert, when he was the leader of our chapel singing, he used to stand looking down into the valley from the highest point of the road, I have seen him do it, wearing his shabby old clothes, unbrushed, covered from the brim of his bowler to the lace-holes of his boots with that film of grey flour from the bakehouse. He would take the tuning-fork out of his waistcoat pocket and sing softly in that beautiful voice of his, a disciplined baritone, magnificent, of great range and sweetness. Every week, whatever the weather, at that last bend in the road before it drops down into the next valley, he drew the cart into the side and hobbled across to look down into the *cwm* and over there at the hills on the far side. What he loved was to see the whole valley unobscured by rain or mist or darkness and lit by the bright sun of the morning. I heard him speak of it often in prayer meeting ; he saw there, in the sunlight, the landscape of his favourite hymns, where his Saviour stood among myrtles, or strode out of Edom conquering, more lovely than the breaking of the dawn.

But, humming to himself softly, his eyes shut, as I have seen him, he must often have forgotten the valley also, and its desolation, being a devout man he was carried away by the poetry of our hymns and the splendour of the promises to us of divine forgiveness. He saw, in a blaze of lightning, a stander upon a lonely rock, as Ehedydd Iâl the poet says, his flesh grass and his bones clay, praising God for the forgiveness of sins while the rivers of blood froth round his crag and drink the hissing lightnings. In Dafydd Morris there was always a streak of unworldliness and dreaming, Mr. Herbert. I can imagine him, and indeed he has told us of it in the *seiat*, standing there alone above the valley in the sun, oblivious in a sort of holy trance, and being awakened by suddenly hearing the old horse behind him tearing grass out of the verge with his teeth. He opened his eyes then and recognised with a shock his dilapidated cart, with *D. Morris, Grocer and Baker* painted on it, and Captain, the big black funeral horse, awkward and un-groomed, between the shafts.

But, as I have told you, Dafydd had not always earned his living as a grocer. Many years ago, when we worked in the mine together, he had loved music, and that, Mr. Herbert, seems the only interest in him which has survived from those youthful and unregenerate days. Music absorbed him. Arguing, as we squatted underground in the pit, eating our meal from our tin food boxes by the light of a ring of our safety lamps standing on the ground, he used to illustrate his points with the staves of old notation chalked on the pit timbers around us supporting the roof, or on the polished underneath of his steel curling box. I was only a boy then, but I remember it well. And he sang regularly in the public houses after work. At night people on this hillside left their kitchen doors open to hear Dafydd Morris singing at the crossroads after the public houses had been turned out. He was negligent of himself but never vicious, the passion of his life seemed to be for singing and comradeship and applause, and with the improvident and drunken among the miners he was popular. I remember when he carried off the baritone solo at Blaennant, an important *eisteddfod* at that time—I remember that a group of men of this rough drinking type collected among themselves to give him an additional prize and presented the money in the gaudy red velvet bag with ribbons on it, and embroidered with his initials, that was often used then in *eisteddfodau*. And if time allows, tonight, Mr. Herbert, I will perhaps have reason to mention that bag again.

But now, about that time, that spirit—excuse me, Mr. Herbert, for some reason your own communion was untouched by it—that spirit, divine and incalculable, of religious revival, entered the valley. Dafydd Morris shared of course the universal curiosity and one night he went with his jeering friends to watch the scenes of seething emotionalism that took place night after night in the crowded chapels of Ystrad. There, I am told, he sat in silence. He did not weep, or beat his breast, or confess his sins aloud or kneel publicly in prayer as many did, but he came out into the crowd on the road outside the chapel changed and sobered. In work, and at home too, we were told, he became silent and absorbed. During the incessant discussions at the coal face of the triumphs and the follies of the revival he would say nothing. He did not visit any further meetings but his friends were quick to notice that singing appeared to be losing something of its domination over him.

But this period was not all uncertainty and bewilderment. One evening when he came home dirty from his work in the pit, he prepared, as usual, for his bath on the hearth-rug before the kitchen fire. Stripped to the waist he lifted down the big iron saucepan off the hob and poured it out steaming on top of the cold water into the wooden tub. Then he knelt down absently and began with a cloth to swill the dirt off his arms and chest. Just then his wife came into the kitchen and began scolding him, poor soul, calling him a fool, not a quarter sane, and so on. And her anger, indeed, Mr. Herbert, was perhaps this time excusable ; because what Dafydd had emptied into the bath tub was the broth for his dinner, and his washing water was still on the hob warming in another of the great saucepans.

And then one evening he suffered the baptism of hatred and ignominy. As he was wandering, alone and unhappy, down there above the weir, he met half a dozen of his friends on their way back home from town. They had been drinking of course and they began their teasing at once, questioning him, jeering, with an undercurrent of malice and even drunken savagery in what they said. But to all their jibes Dafydd answered patiently, that was always his way, but he steadily refused to promise to sing for them again. Then they became angry, accusing him of ingratitude, desertion, the neglect of old friendships. Twm Gravell, the fitter, an amateur heavyweight he was, with the frame of a giant—Twm lost his temper at the calm and reasonableness of Dafydd's answers. "Boys," he said —excuse the language I am about to use, Mr. Herbert, if you please, it is Twm Gravell's and not my own, of course— "Boys," he said, "Mr. Bloody Morris have been converted. Here's the river by here, boys. Let's baptise the sod."

Unresisting, they say, Dafydd was dragged down the steep bank, through the trees and thrown into the river. There, at the weir, the water is deep and he sank out of sight immediately. Rising again further down he clambered up the bank with difficulty and saw the gang running away into the darkness. He went home that night, he told me, Mr. Herbert, in despair, his soul sickened by a sense of loathing at the defilement of flesh and spirit he had endured.

And then one day underground he had his accident. That was the time I damaged this hand of mine working with the rescue party to free the men who had been trapped—a late rock fell out of the roof and crushed my finger here to a batter on my shovel handle. But that is by the way.

In spite of the jeers of Twm Gravell and his sort, Mr. Herbert, Dafydd was not quite a convert yet, one of the 'people of the certainty,' as we say ; although, filled with remorse and a sense of unworthiness, he was, as you will recognize, with his face in the direction of the light. Then came the terrible accident. He was cutting coal that day in the nine-foot seam, where we were working together at the time—and I ought to tell you, Mr. Herbert, that Dafydd, a powerful man, was a fine collier, and when he attacked the face the coal came boiling out under his pick—as I say, working in the Rhas Las nine-foot seam, he heard the top above him dribbling stones, a sign of a coming roof fall, but before he could jump clear the whole ceiling, twenty yards of rock, came down in dust and thunder around him. His leap, although it failed to land him in safety, at least brought him to the edge of the fall, so that, instead of finding him completely buried when we at last groped our way to him, we saw him by our lamps pinned down by masses of rock from chest to feet ; he lay there unconscious, the whole of his lower body held under an immovable burden, under tons of rock and rubble.

After working feverishly by the light of our colliers' lamps we at last got him free and took him, crushed and bleeding profusely, to the surface. He had regained consciousness by then. But from that accident and the ordeal of the journey to the pit-shaft that followed it, his shattered legs and feet never recovered. With one arm around my shoulders and one round Jim Rice's, both of us shorter than he was, Dafydd swung in agony between us as we made for the parting and the pit bottom and the cage. He was conscious of the weight of his great bulk upon us and he tried, from time to time, groaning, with sweat pouring off him, to place his crushed feet on the ground to lessen our burden. But the agony of it was unendurable. And I remember another terrible thing during that journey. At intervals, in the darkness, his dangling legs cracked against the steel rollers in between the tram-rails over which the tram ropes ran ; and with the agony of those blows he screamed out loud and passed into unconsciousness again on our shoulders. With the pain and throbbing of my own hand and the memory of that journey I lay awake night after night, unable to sleep, I used to hear in my bed those nightmare howls, Dafydd Morris's voice echoing in agony among the hollow headings as his smashed legs crashed into the unseen metal rollers.

And Dafydd lay in bed too, month after month, in their little back bedroom, sometimes in great pain, sometimes in the merciful stupor of drugs. Both his legs were broken and his pelvis utterly smashed. It was evident that, even if he was to live at all, he would never work in the pit again. And in his physical agony and his mood of spiritual distress none of his visitors was more welcome than the vigorous old minister of his childhood's chapel, William Morgans, Bethesda, a grim old man, from whose presence as children at least, Mr. Herbert, we used to run away. He was short in figure and thickish, as I remember him, heavily, perhaps, some would say, even grossly built. His long pale face and the front of his neck were hung with plentiful loose skin and he had a shining skullcap of close-cropped silver hair. His nose, marked blue across the high crest with the scar of the coalminer, was arrogant, as was the glance of his large light eyes. His expression was always bold and authoritative, it had pride of mission and lofty dedication, and no church-prince, I used to think, could be more jealous than he was of the dignity and awesomeness of his calling. He worshipped the Saviour who blasted the fig-tree, and foretold for his followers the sword, who declared that the fruitless branch should be cast out into the fire, who drove out the money-changers from the Temple with the twisted cords. But Dafydd Morris found in the narrow pride and fearlessness of this upright old man some strange restoration and strength. Together they used to sit in the plain little bedroom watching through the window the scene in the valley below them and opposite them, the bare stretches of hillside grassland, the coloured gardens of the miners, the funnels of the anchored pit steaming into the sunlight.

Sometimes, when Dafydd was well enough, they talked. Morgans cared nothing for the graces of conversation, he cared nothing for music either, or for discussions about it. Dafydd Morris's voice, the finest in five valleys then, he judged as the dust of scale-pans ; and indeed he seemed almost insensitive, Dafydd often told me, to the suffering of that broken and emaciated body lying before him. His large glowing eyes were turned upon Dafydd in challenge rather than in tenderness and compassion. For him the big helpless man upon the bed was far more than flesh and bone in physical agony, he was the possessor of an immortal soul which might be saved and, with God's help, he, William Morgans, would defy all hell to save it.

I was several times visiting in that little bedroom where Dafydd had to lie. It was clean and simple because Hannah Morris, with all her faults—and she had many, poor soul, as you shall hear, Mr. Herbert—Hannah was a good housewife then. There was a black iron bedstead in it, a red chair, a red washstand, a red door. The wallpaper had faded almost white, and a pink oilcloth patterned with bunches of red roses covered the floor. Later on, when Dafydd was recovering, we went there regularly to teach him to walk again, and we used those bunches of roses to mark his improvement from lesson to lesson—one week he would manage to totter on his crutches past two of the bunches, the next week past three, and so on.

Always a little fire burned in the grate, and on the black iron mantelpiece above it stood three or four silver cups and a few plush-lined cases with the medals in them Dafydd had won singing at various *eisteddfodau* in the valleys. The red velvet pocket I spoke of earlier, presented by his public house friends, was also there, hanging above the trophies by its yellow ribbon from a glass-headed pin stuck into the wall-paper. And it was in that bedroom, as I have often heard him describe, that the events occurred which brought him for the time peace, and restored him to the community from which the heedlessness and irresponsibility of his youth, he felt deeply, had for a long time exiled him.

It was a fine day in spring, the sun in panes of light on the white bed coverlet, a heavy fly buzzing against the window. Outside Dafydd could see his neglected garden full of willow-herb, the wet fence steaming in the sun, the bare hills, and the blue sky. But for all its beauty the day was a bitter one for him. The doctor had that morning told him that amputation of one or both his legs might after all be necessary.

As he lay in bed tears of bitterness and rebellion broke from his lids. The old preacher, on one of his visits, was seated in his thick black clothes with the braided edges beside the bed, the sun silvering the plush of his clipped skull-cap. He gazed down dour and unmoved at the weeping man, watching in silence the tears coursing down the scooped out cheeks. And then Dafydd caught sight of the velvet bag hanging from its glass-headed pin half-way up the chimney breast, and at the sight of it, he says, he felt some strange lightening of his grief, for the moment his heart was less heavy and in the middle of his tears a faint smile appeared on his lips.

The old minister frowned and turned and followed the direction of Dafydd's gaze. His large beaming eyes fell upon the medals and the cups and the gaudy velvet bag hanging high above them with the letters *D.M.* worked crudely in gold thread upon it. Could it be this object which had brought remission to the face of the sufferer, the momentary respite and comfort ? What was it ? He left the red chair and went heavily across to the fireplace and took the crude red pocket in his hands.

"What is this, Dafydd Morris ?" he asked. "Your initials ?"

"It's a prize bag, a present given me long ago," Dafydd answered, pushing away his tears in shame with the back of his hand.

"It was perhaps given you for singing ?"

"Yes. I had it for singing."

"Where did you win it ?"

"In the next valley. In Blaennant."

"That *eisteddfod*," said the old man, "is a big one. It surprises me they should present you with such a bag."

He fingered the tawdry red object with his thick lower lip pushed out in contempt and distaste. "Shoddy. Unworthy," he muttered.

"It was presented to me," Dafydd explained, "to acknowledge my win. Some of my friends gave it to me. My first big singing victory."

The watchful eyes of the old man kindled, he lifted up his head with an affronted expression on his face.

"What friends ?" he asked.

Dafydd hesitated and flushed. "Huw Reece," he said, "Twm Gravell, Steve Williams, Joe Phillips, those."

Morgans tossed the bag on to the bed as though he had suffered defilement. "Friends, did you say ?" he asked coming forward and standing above the bed. "Friends ? Blasphemers who jeered at you, thwarted you, who cast you in your weakness into the river. Wantoners, fornicators. Evil livers who employed all the devices of Satan to drag you back from the circle of the promise, towards which, God be praised, you had turned your face. Friends, did you say ? You can call them friends after the usages of this world, but answer me this, how many of them, since you have lain helpless in this bed, have had the grace to visit you ?"

Even in his unhappiness a half smile appeared on Dafydd's face. "Well, all of them," he answered. "They have all been here some time or another, shaking hands and hoping that everything was all right between us."

The old man's eyes blazed. "It were to your advantage," he said flushed and in anger, "if they had never set foot over the threshold, if in shame and repentance they had stayed away." He glanced down at the bed. "This bag," he said, "it must be destroyed. Cast it from you as a symbol of a life you have repented of, which you have forsaken and abjured for ever."

"No, no," Dafydd pleaded, the sweat thick on his forehead. "Don't let me destroy it. It was given to me in kindness. Don't let it be destroyed, wantonly."

"Dafydd Morris," said the masterful old man, "it must be destroyed. Take hold of the evil thing. Cast it into the fire."

He fixed his imperious hypnotic stare upon Dafydd's face. To him the fate of the gaudy little velvet bag had become of eternal moment, the tiny room was a battleground and around the beribboned pocket was being waged the final struggle for the soul of this dying collier. He gathered up all the authority and masterfulness of his powerful nature while the sick man hesitated.

"Dafydd Morris," he said in the rich Welsh of his westward birthplace, "Dafydd Morris, I command you now, in the name of Almighty God, in the name of Christ our Lord and Saviour, in the name of the cloud of witnesses and the holy dead, I command you, in the name of everything sacred to you here upon earth and in heaven above, now, in this room, to renounce and abjure your life, I command you to come forth, I command you to burn, root out, destroy, every vestige of your sin. I command you, as the servant of the Eternal God I command you, to forsake sighing, backward glancing, the damnation of Lot's wife, and come away. And let this be the token and symbol of your submission and repentance."

He picked up the red bag again off the bed and thrust it into the sick man's hands. Dafydd looked at it for a moment, glanced up desperately at the gross and menacing bulk of the old minister and tossed it weakly towards the fire. Through the feebleness of the throw it fell short but the old man picked it up off the rug and pitched it contemptuously on to the glowing coals. At once the dried-up velvet broke into a flame that went up the chimney like a golden rope. Dafydd's head fell back and he passed into the unconsciousness of exhaustion.

Mr. Jeffreys stopped speaking and we halted a moment to look down from the mountain into the darkness of the valley now far below us. There we could see our town, well defined by the street lights clustered in handfuls and stretched out into long chains in the night. The weather was clearer now, the darkness was warm and soft about us and we stood side by side a few minutes in silence. Then somewhere in the town below an engine sighed and the metallic clink of shunted trucks came distinctly up to us, and we moved on again in the direction of the top of the mountain.

I have not said much yet, Mr. Herbert, Mr. Jeffreys went on, about Hannah Morris, the wife of Dafydd Morris, but now I ought to tell you one or two things about her because without her Dafydd's story would no doubt be very different from what it is. Dafydd always spoke of her to the end with tenderness and affection, especially of their life together before they came to the shop. And no doubt, with her glossy hair, and her flashing black eyes and her unhampered movements, she must have been a fascinating young woman to a man of Dafydd's temperament. But how difficult life is to foresee. Perhaps if her lap had felt the tread of children she would not have been so completely set upon money and possessions. She was, Mr. Herbert, without any doubt, the one with energy and decision, in her nature there was no room for the hesitancies of sentiment or any scruples. According to her own lights she was, no doubt, just, but her righteousness as time went on became grim and cold and unlovely.

I remember Dafydd saying to me once, at the time I started visiting Lowri, "When I was courting Hannah, Robert, I used to go up to their house on a Saturday evening when her mother had gone out shopping, and watch her knitting or mending clothes by the table in the kitchen, or making apple tart for their tea on Sunday. She had a fine hand for pastry always, as you know. One thing especially I thought amusing and charming in her in those days, although I could never explain why. When she was cutting up the cooking apples to put them in the tart she would never peel them, and when I saw her under the clear lamplight slicing apples on to the pastry covering the bottom of the plate, with the skin still bright green and shining like silk on them, the novelty was something magical to me, it used to give me a delightful sensation of enchantment almost, because I had never seen that done before." A strange thing for a man to speak about so long after. What do you think of it, Mr. Herbert?

Undoubtedly the shop was the corruptor of her character, although I think the weakness of greed was within her before. Do you know that in the end she had become so grasping that Dafydd had to pay for every stick of barley sugar he took out with him on his rounds? And she used to charge herself too for the pinch of cloves taken into the kitchen for her apple tart? And for what, Mr. Herbert? For what?

But let me try to tell you what she had become, from something I saw myself in the shop one day—greedy, sharp-tongued, suspicious, and yet with some attraction about her for Dafydd in spite of her faults. Let me piece together what I was a witness of and what I heard from Phoebe Francis and Willy her husband, and Maldwyn Edwards the assistant in the *Crown Stores*. And Dafydd himself also.

Imagine Phoebe Francis, now, Mr. Herbert, a shabby old woman she was, coming slowly along the pavement of Station Street; she walks beside the high brick retaining wall of the railway embankment opposite the *Crown Stores*. She is dressed as she always was, all in black, wearing a man's cloth cap pinned on through the bun at the back of her head, a large woollen shawl, a heavy skirt, patched, and laced-up boots showing her poor bunions. Her name, Mr. Herbert, as I think I told you, was Phoebe Francis, and she would earn a few pence from her neighbours for washing their bed-clothes or doing a bit of paper-hanging, or laying out a corpse, and some called her the Jews' Poker, because for a copper or two she would poke up the fires for the religious Jews on their Sabbath. Poor Phoebe, her face was always flabby and colourless, her nose swollen, covered with a network of red veins. She was a bit simple-minded, really, I suppose, her expression,

24

poor thing, was always harassed and resentful and, I must say, a bit crafty as well.

I was in the *Crown Stores* when I saw her standing by the retaining brickwork on the opposite side of the street. She pulled her shawl around her and then started fingering the brooch at her throat. She crossed the road towards the shop and peeped in through the window, I could see her over the purple-stamped hams and dishes of bacon. Then, satisfied with her examination, she came down the steps into the shop where at the moment I was the only customer.

"Where is *she* ?" she whispered to the young man behind the bacon counter. *She*, of course, Mr. Herbert, could only be Mrs. Morris.

The shop assistant was Maldwyn Edwards, tall and bald, in his white starched apron and jacket with the comb in the breast pocket. That was Maldwyn all over, Mr. Herbert, a real wag he was and a loss to this valley when he died. His blue eyes were brilliant, I can see them now, they used to flicker all the time with mischief. He bared the hard toothless gums he had, grinning, stripping off the wooden box from around the big fifty six pound butter block on the counter. "It's all right, Phoebe," he said. "She's gone into the warehouse. What can I do for you ?"

The old woman stood by one of the iron pillars holding up the roof beams. Dafydd always used to paper these pillars with coloured labels, so that the roof seemed to be supported by columns of salmon tins or tins of golden syrup. "Wanted to ask you I did, to pin this brooch for me, Maldwyn *bach*," she said. "It happened to come out jest as I was passing."

Maldwyn leaned over the counter still grinning and fastened the big brooch back into the cross-over shawl. "There you are, Phoebe," he said. "Now, what next ?"

"Thank you indeed, Maldwyn," she said, patting her throat. "That's better. There's nothing else I wanted, thank you. I only wanted for you to fasten the brooch, because my hands are shaking so bad." She looked up at the green tea canisters on the shelves behind him for a moment. "I suppose you couldn't spare us a bit of firewood, like, could you ?" she asked. "I haven't got a bit of anything I can put the chopper into in the house."

Maldwyn stooped and pulled out a few strips of the white butter-box he had just thrown under the counter. "Will this do?" he said. "Put them under your shawl now before anybody comes. How is Willy there with you now?" he went on, grinning. "Is he any better these days?"

Willy, as I told you, Mr. Herbert, was Phoebe's husband, a workshy if ever there was one. He was supposed to be suffering from nystagmus and you could often see him standing in the middle of the road shading his eyes and peering anxiously up at the town clock to see if it was getting near time for the pubs to open.

"No indeed, Maldwyn *bach*," the old woman said. "When our Willy's legs are better his arms are worse, and when he haven't got the earick his bowels are upset or there's something the matter with his kidneys. I am daunted, indeed there." She took a sixpence out of her purse and very thoughtfully scooped a long groove up the side of the block of butter with it. "You couldn't let me have an ounce of shag on strap for him now, could you, Maldwyn? Only an ounce, like," she added, licking the butter off the sixpence.

Maldwyn's blue eyes sparkled. "No indeed I couldn't, Phoebe," he said. "If the misses found out I'd given you anything on account the waggon would be in the ditch, I can tell you that. She's not a-willing, see."

"She's a proper old screw, she is," Phoebe said. "I hope one day she'll be down on the bones of her behind worse than me and our Willy is. I suppose I better go now before I do see her, or I will be sure to give her the rough side of my tongue. So long now, Maldwyn *bach*, and thank you for the firewood. You don't mind me asking, like, do you?"

"So long, Phoebe," Maldwyn answered, picking up the claw hatchet to go on with his stripping. "Come again."

The old woman was pulling herself up the steps to reach the pavement when Hannah Morris came into the shop from the warehouse.

"Phoebe Francis," she said, "stop a minute, will you?"

Phoebe turned round on the middle step. Hannah was

standing at the back of the shop with a ledger under her arm. She was by then a small jet-haired woman, juiceless and swarthy ; she dressed in black, wore a long thin gold chain and seemed soured by everything she saw through her gold rimmed glasses.

"Hullo, Mrs. Morris," said Phoebe. "I didn't notice you by there. How are you keeping, girl ?"

"Never mind how I'm keeping," Mrs. Morris answered. "Listen here ! Have you got a bit of salt with you ?"

"Salt ?" said Phoebe, not moving, standing up there near the doorway. "Salt, Hannah Morris, did you say ? How do you mean *salt* ? What do you think I want salt for, say you ?"

"For this," Mrs. Morris said, holding the ledger out before her and tapping the cover with her finger-nail. "To rub into your account, Phoebe Francis. It's started stinking."

The old woman stared down at her for a moment from the steps without saying a word. Then she turned and went on climbing in silence up out of the shop. When she reached the pavement she turned again and kicked the sawdust off her boots against the doorpost. "Keep your flaming firewood," she shouted, taking the strips of butter-box from under her shawl and throwing them back down on to the floor of the shop. "Keep it. I'd rather freeze than use anything from this flaming place. Our Willy said the softest part of you is your teeth, and he's not far wrong neither. And I hope one day when you put your hand down on the floor of your pocket you won't find nothing there, like me and our Willy. Keep your flaming firewood, you skingey old sow."

She turned away and went off up the street, muttering and pulling her big shawl tighter around her. Before she had gone many yards she came face to face with Dafydd Morris hurrying out of the bakehouse next door and occupying most of the pavement as usual with his roll. They spoke and Phoebe went on her way calmer. "Don't be hard on Hannah, Phoebe *fach*, there's a good girl," Dafydd said in his gentle way. "I will bring an ounce of shag round tonight after closing. Say nothing. There is some fault on all of us, and a certain weakness for money is Hannah's, perhaps. Perhaps. Don't be hard on her, there's a good girl."

27

Back in the shop Maldwyn expected the storm, I could see that, and he began humming *Crugybar* to himself. "None of that," Mrs. Morris snapped, glaring over her glasses. "And don't let me have to tell you again about handing fire-wood out. We've got to *sell* things in this shop, not *give* them away. You didn't give the slut any account, did you ?"

Maldwyn shook his bald head, silent and stubborn. She studied him a moment but he ignored her, he went on using the claw on the two stone of butter. She stepped across to the box with the tobacco in, on the counter, made up into tubular half-ounce packets. As she was examining them her husband appeared on the top step at the street door, large and awkward, dimming the shop.

He spoke a word to me and then he asked where Harry was. Harry was his friend, Mr. Herbert, he called in at the *Crown Stores* for a chat every day and I will tell you more about him presently.

"Where's Harry ?" he said. "Hasn't he been in ? I met him up the street and he said he was calling."

"No," Hannah answered. "Not yet." Then she went on sharply, "I'm checking these half-ounces," she said. "They're still the same so far. I did wonder if Phoebe Francis was the one. I'll catch him though, whoever he is. I won't be bested by a thief, I'm telling you. A half-ounce packet every week for over a month now, sometimes two. But I'll catch him, you see if I don't."

Dafydd looked down at her with troubled eyes. This was a hateful thing to him. "How will you do that, Hannah *fach* ?" he asked soothingly, with a sort of pleading in his voice. "I expect you miscounted them."

"No, I haven't miscounted them. I've made sure of that. I'll lay a trap for him, don't you worry. And if I catch him I'll prosecute him too, don't you fret now."

Dafydd shuffled through the sawdust into the warehouse at the back and I saw the glance of understanding that passed between him and Maldwyn on his way.

What I have been telling you now, Mr. Herbert, this last small episode, took place, let me see, about fifteen years ago, just before Dafydd Morris received from us what he considered high honour, the highest, even. His throwing into the fire of the little velvet bag, which I tried to describe to you just now, was for him the complete gesture of renunciation and conversion. Regularly after that, when he was able to walk again, I saw him towering among the baritones on the gallery of Bethesda, and then, when Thomas the Leader died, Dafydd became the conductor of the chapel choir. He performed this task faithfully for twenty years, he was beautiful at it, gentle and persuasive, and his only fault, in my opinion, was too great a leniency towards those who were indifferent and irregular in their attendance at singing school. But then Dafydd's purpose in this world, he had chosen it, was to be the long sufferer ; the neck of Abel, as I heard that preacher saying, rather than the knife of Cain.

And acknowledgement of his devotion during this time grew to be universal in the valley, and the stories of Dafydd's youth were forgotten or not believed. And as a mark of this regard for him the honour I mentioned just now was conferred upon him.

I know you have learnt, Mr. Herbert, that the chapels in this valley hold at Easter an united religious singing festival, a *gymanfa ganu*. The conductor for this is customarily a guest from a distance, someone of acknowledged musical standing in our country. But about ten, fifteen, years ago, as I say, Dafydd Morris was invited to conduct this annual *gymanfa* in his own valley. At first, from feelings of unworthiness, he declined, but there were many persuasive tongues on that *gymanfa* committee and finally Dafydd consented.

I remember very well the Easter Tuesday of the festival, a day of triumph for Dafydd Morris. The meetings were always held in Saron, the largest chapel in the Ystrad Valley, and that, in the evening, was crowded. I was recovering from my annual quinsy at the time and so I had to find a seat downstairs for once, and not with the choir on the gallery.

While the chairman was speaking before the singing of the final chorus I watched Dafydd Morris occupying the conductor's armchair up there in the high pulpit, prominent in the downbeam of the lamp hung just above his head ; and it was plain to me that he sat there in fulfilment and blessedness, the expression on his face was one of complete serenity as he looked about at his choir in the chapel galleries to his right and left and before him. No clapping of hands is permitted in our chapels, of course, but during that packed out meeting the conductor had other proofs and assurances of the regard of his audience. The people had sat in enthralled stillness during hymn after hymn, during anthem after anthem, although as I say the chapel was crowded. In fact the building was so full that chairs had to be carried into the aisles, and both the stairways leading up to the gallery were packed with a solid mass of people who had arrived too late to get a seat inside the building. There were even people sitting crowded together on the window-sills. But in spite of all this, the discomfort, the perspiring, the stifling air, the attention of the people to the end was strict and undiminished. And Dafydd Morris knew it was so.

Dafydd was dressed, as I saw him under that glaring lamp, in his conducting clothes, the black suit of evening dress he wore for his engagements, with a bit of satin shining on the lapels of his jacket, a white collar attached to a breast, and a black tucked-under bow-tie. As he sat, with a sort of radiance upon him, under that downward light, I watched him, as I said, glancing round during the chairman's praises, fiddling with the buttons of his waistcoat ; tin trouser buttons they were, Mr. Herbert, half of them, because when the cloth ones came off, Hannah was too mean, gone, to buy him new ones. After she went to the shop she cared nothing at all for the way Dafydd faced the world. She sent him out on his bread-rounds looking like a scarecrow, only dusty with flour, and you could tell by a glance at his shirt collar that by then she hadn't much interest in the flat-iron. And yet, when he was underground, it was a pleasure to see him going to work, with tidy white duck patches on the knees of his pit-trousers, and the duck cap she had made for him, and the wide belt of duck for slinging his box-and-jack over his shoulder.

But no matter for that now. The response of Dafydd's choir throughout the day, as I have said, had been warm and wholehearted, and his happiness in them was complete. He glanced round again and again with affection at the altos

30

and sopranos seated in the wooden pews of the gallery above him, at the tenors and basses up against the green streaming walls of the chapel. He smiled and I smiled with him, at the earnestness of the singers, at Mrs. Rees Top-notes ; at Clara Central Cottages who claimed she could only read her music in old notation and half her time held her copy upside down ; at Bryn Chin stuttering the anthems out of his enormous jaw— "That sittetheth upon the thro-one, that sittetheth upon the throne" ; at Lewis the Graig, the grumbler, complaining, as I remember him, every week in singing school, "Lev us rise, now will you, Dafydd Morris ? Lev us rise. Us been sitting by 'ere now for two hours, aye, singing these pieces. Lev us rise a bit, like, now, will you ?"

Daylight had not left the sky when that evening part of the *gymanfa* began, and the crowded chapel was filled with golden light. It was pleasant to hear the black linen blinds that hung over the open windows making that clicking noise as the evening breeze puffed them forward into the chapel and then sucked them back again. But by the time the last chorus was to be sung all the lights in the building were lit and I could see stars shining through the curved uncovered fanlights above the window blinds.

The chairman sat down at last and Dafydd, picking up the ivory baton the choir had presented to him, lifted his big clumsy bulk out of the pulpit armchair. The *gymanfa* was almost at an end. The organ commenced the vibrating introduction to the ' Hallelujah Chorus,' traditionally sung by us, Mr. Herbert, as perhaps you know, to terminate our Easter *cymanfaoedd*. The choir rose and the audience crowding the floor of the chapel rose also to join in, as was always done. Dafydd Morris conducted this singing like one inspired. His face there in the lamp's downbeam I shall never forget. ' King of Kings, and Lords of Lords ! And He shall reign for ever and ever ! ' The exultation of the music filled him, he seemed uplifted with a sense of the majesty of God, and the tenderness of His love, and with his own blissful identification with the singing around him.

And then, in the middle of that chorus, an alarming and revealing thing happened. As everyone, choir and audience together, was singing the great *laus Deo*, the electric wire from the high chapel roof, from which the pulpit-light which shone down on Dafydd Morris hung, burst into flames, and the lamp with its large metal shade, narrowly missing him, crashed on to the table in the big seat below. There the flaring wire was quickly put out and no damage was done. But the strange thing was that so absorbed and uplifted was Dafydd Morris that he appeared not to notice at all what had happened, he remained unconscious in his ecstasy both of the great blue flare hissing down past his eyes and the loud crash which followed it. And the singing, in response to his triumphant mood, proceeded with unalterable movement and feeling. The only thing changed was this—during the latter part of the chorus, that expressive face was no longer illuminated from above to a bright transparency, Dafydd's conducting was carried on instead in the ordinary and equalised light of the chapel.

After the *gymanfa* had finished, he told me later, he remembered little of what had happened, he had a sense of universal congratulation, of smiles and hand-claspings, but his feeling of triumph and identity and exaltation obliterated all particular impressions and he took to his house an inward illumination of peace and joy.

Mr. Jeffreys and I had by this time reached the cross-roads made by the intersection of the old Roman way running over the hill into the next valley. The wind was high and we stood for a minute or two again, looking down into the valley. From that height, nearly at the top of the mountain, we could see great distances. The risen moon, curved and glassy, sailed by in the glare of her own light. I felt a strange sense of fulfilment and elation.

I ought to begin to tell you now, Mr. Herbert, Mr. Jeffreys said as we started our steep descent back into the town, about Harry the Boot, a very well-known and very engaging character in this valley at the time I am talking of. He was a littlish humped man, something like a hairless monkey to look at, but with big ears of a bright yellow colour, the lobes very fleshy, and hanging loose. His face was heavily wrinkled and covered with dark brown speckles but his bald head, on the other hand, had a tight polished look. He had no human dignity, or even self-respect, as the foolish eager sort of grin on his face showed plainly.

Harry's real style was Jones, I think, but everybody called him by this other name because he had been brought up in a house that had once been a public house, the ' Boot Inn.' Some people held that Harry was just simple and amusing, others said there was real cunning hidden under his comicality. I don't know. It was hard to tell which.

For instance now, when he was a lout of a boy he often used to come to our home on a Saturday afternoon to call for Emlyn, my eldest brother, to go to the football match together. One Saturday my mother said to him, "Em hasn't come home from work yet, Harry. Are you going to wait for him ? You can sit down in there if you like." Harry said yes, he'd wait, so my mother put him in the middle room out of the way. "Would you like a cup of tea ?" she said to him. "And there's a plate of rhubarb tart on the table if you want some." With that my mother, always busy with eight of us to bring up, went back to her work in the kitchen, leaving Harry on his own with an uncut plate of tart and a cup of tea before him. When she passed through the room a quarter of an hour later all that was left of that rhubarb tart was the tin plate and one thin slice no wider than your finger. My mother looked at him, flushed and very surprised, and Harry was quick to excuse himself. "I'm very sorry indeed, Mrs. Jeffreys," he said, "but I *couldn't* eat it all, I've done my best, but I *had* to leave that little piece behind." Was that simple-mindedness, Mr. Herbert, or cunning ? I don't know which.

But I do believe that after his accident any eccentricity or moral weakness or disorder in him was intensified. He used to work on top of the pit and one night as he was walking home along the railway line in pitch darkness, the colliers' train came up behind him, hit him flat between the rails and ran over him. Fortunately for him he was carrying a log of firewood over his shoulder at the time, so that his body did not receive the full impact of the engine ; and also he fell as I say, plumb in between the metals. But his head cracked heavily on the sleepers as he went down and he lay unconscious for several hours before he was found by the men coming on the day shift. He was, after that, I always felt, more unstable and unpredictable, in short, speaking with all charity, dafter than he was before, and as he grew older the differences between him and the rest of us became more and more marked.

But his wrongheadedness, Mr. Herbert, please don't mistake me, was innocent and endearing, almost everyone looked upon him as a harmless droll and from one end of the valley to the other people welcomed him and teased him and laughed at him. "Why are you calling Tommy Carter your cousin, Harry ?" I said to him once. "I didn't know Tommy was related to you." "Well no, Robert," he said with his puckered-up monkey-grin. "We're not related proper, like, but the wife had a child by him before we was married." That will show you, Mr. Herbert, the sort of world Harry inhabited.

Dafydd Morris had a great liking for Harry. It was Harry, I might say, he always asked for when he came back into the shop after his bread-round. Hardly a day passed but the two met. And there in the *Crown Stores* with Dafydd smiling at him and Maldwyn Edwards egging him on, poor Harry made some of his most famous jokes, the ones that people in the valley at one time used to pass on from one to another. But now, it was through him that tragedy came upon Dafydd Morris. I hinted, didn't I, some time back, that Hannah Morris was determined to set a trap to catch the thief who was stealing her half-ounce packets of tobacco ? Harry the Boot turned out to be the thief. I am afraid, Mr. Herbert, as you shall hear, that there could be no question about his guilt, poor dab.

Without telling anyone, Mrs. Morris carried out her threat. What she did was to cut about a yard of the white string they used for packing in the *Crown Stores* and tuck one end of it very firmly into one of the paper packets of tobacco. She put the packet back into the box on the counter with the others and hid the length of string underneath very cleverly, so that it could not be noticed. A day or two later Harry was in the shop as usual, Maldwyn was provoking him and he was talking with that comical wrong-headedness that people used to like so much to hear. But when it was all over and he was

34

making his way up out of the shop, still laughing and joking, Mrs. Morris came in from the warehouse. She called him back in her abrupt way, exactly as she had done with Phoebe Francis. When he came down to the bottom step she said, "What is that string hanging out of your coat pocket, Harry ? Come here, let me have a look. You don't happen to have half an ounce of tobacco on the other end of it, do you ? Let's see !"

She thrust her hand into Harry's coat pocket and pulled out half an ounce of tobacco with the string tied on to it.

Harry, poor fellow, was terrified, he broke down, his face was white, like something peeled, he confessed and pleaded for mercy as though he was hysterical. All the instability and suppressed terror of his nature came out then ; he was, so Maldwyn told me, like someone demented with fear, he cringed on the floor, he cried out loud, and sobbed in remorse, there was pandemonium in the shop as Hannah described in her cold mocking way what was soon to happen to him.

Dafydd was out on his rounds at the time and Harry had been taken home a long time when he arrived at the shop again that night. He was greatly troubled at what had happened, all his concern was for the unhappiness of poor Harry. He assumed that nothing further was to happen to him. But Hannah—there was this strange hardness and malevolence about her, Mr. Herbert—Hannah told him that the matter was already in the hands of the police.

It is painful for me, Mr. Herbert, even now, to speak of all the details of this episode, and I will not do it. But from what happened in the next week or two Dafydd Morris never recovered, nor ever will this side of the grave. For Harry did not make that appearance he so much dreaded before the police court. He shot himself. A day or two before the case was to be called the poor frenzied creature went up to his brother-in-law's house, smuggled a shot-gun out into the garden shed and destroyed himself with it. He was found sitting on the stool with the gun between his knees and nine inches of the barrel driven up into his head from under his chin with the kick of the discharge. Poor terrified mortal. And all for the sake of half an ounce of tobacco that Dafydd

35

would have given him willingly for nothing. Why did he pilfer in this way, Mr. Herbert ? He could have meant no harm to Dafydd, his friend, but did he, in some confused way, imagine that he was spiting Hannah for all her meanness ? The workings of a mind like his are difficult to follow, I have found.

But my concern is with Dafydd Morris. After the shooting his silence and absorption were pitiful. He went about like one haunted. In a short time he gave up his bread round and hired a man to do it for him ; and soon he was seldom going beyond the warehouse at all. He withdrew into himself and on the road he passed his friends hurriedly with a dry nod, as though he feared that given the opportunity they might treat him in the same way. He didn't seek people out to repeat his story to them, or embarrass strangers with long protestations of his innocence, as I have seen many doing obsessed with grief or injury or injustice. There was something aloof and withdrawn about him always and I cannot think of him pouncing upon anyone like some, and diving into his inside pockets for documents to prove his case. His suffering was solitary and incommunicable. His resignation from his position as conductor of our chapel choir we accepted unwillingly, and with protest, but he continued to attend Bethesda on Sundays, slipping in after the service had commenced and leaving during the last hymn. And yet, during that whole time, I do not recall hearing a single word of blame or reproach spoken against Dafydd himself, but only expressions of sympathy rather.

Feeling against Mrs. Morris, on the other hand, was naturally very strong in many quarters, as I shall show you, but for her to arouse antipathy and even hatred among her neighbours was not anything new. During the big stoppage in the coalfield that had only just come to an end at that time she gained many enemies by the bitter way she spoke about the strikers and, worse, her unwillingness to give ' old account ' to her customers. She grudged necessities like cheese and bread to decent, hard working families who had bought their groceries at the *Crown Stores* for years, and who, before the strike, had never been a penny in her debt. She forgot that whatever prosperity she enjoyed had come from the generosity of the colliers who had set Dafydd up in business after his accident. She said openly now that those who refused to work deserved to starve.

In the circumstances Dafydd was able to lessen the harshness of her refusals by private gifts and other kindnesses, and I know that certain classes of people, large families, good singers, those who regularly attended prayer-meeting and so on, were well cared-for by him throughout the strike. But now he was helpless. Rapidly his hair seemed to whiten. His stoop became more marked. He shambled about the valley in his shabby old clothes alone, always silent and brooding, and the lines on his face appeared to deepen and multiply almost from day to day.

And then, about a month after the shooting, something happened which completed the withdrawal into himself that Harry's death had begun.

One sunny Monday morning, as he opened the shop door, he saw in huge letters something written in tar on the long station wall right opposite the *Crown Stores*. You will excuse me, Mr. Herbert, but I cannot lay my tongue to the malice and obscenity of the message that appeared there. The words were about Mrs. Morris and, as I said, they had been roughly printed there on the retaining brickwork with a brush-stump or a tarred stick, in letters two feet high, the whole sentence extended perhaps fifteen or twenty feet across the wall, and the sun shone on it.

The effect of this upon Dafydd was to turn him into a man no longer capable of speech or clear understanding of what was going on around him. Worse, he seemed unable to endure further emotion, he could no longer kindle because his heart was already a cinder. Before he read the tarred message he did attend Bethesda, sitting, as I said, in the backseat or in the ' goats' pen,' but now he did not go out at all on Sundays. Indeed, he was hardly ever to be seen abroad by daylight, he became a night walker, a prowler of the valleys. On two separate occasions at that time someone, late at night, still filled with a terrible unquenchable spirit of hatred and revenge, someone took a shot-gun to the top of the station wall opposite the shop and used it to smash both the plate glass windows of the *Crown Stores*. But this seemed to have no effect on Dafydd

37

now. Friends, neighbours, members of Bethesda, men who had worked underground with him, all of us tried to break through to him with words of comfort, but he could see himself only as an Ishmael, Mr. Herbert, exiled, forsaken, certain that God's love flowed now in different beds.

A year or two later Mrs. Morris died, not of course of a broken heart but of some strange infection of the blood. She had, you may depend, apart from Dafydd, a dry funeral. Dafydd gave up the shop at once and went to live with a niece in the next valley. I thought he would make straight for the grave then, but no, within a few months he was back here and he went into the lodgings he now occupies. And vile lodgings they are. I myself, from the street, have seen the rats inside running across the window-sill of his room. And at night, as I told you, he walks up to Bethesda and sits alone in the gallery, in darkness, sometimes for an hour or two. What do you think, Mr. Herbert, could have broken the heart of this good man? Is it remorse? But for what? Or a sense of unworthiness, or the ache of being cast out from the community of his fellows, or the agony of being abandoned by God? What is it, do you think?

He became silent and we walked on. We were back down in the streets again now and the drizzle began to be dusted down cold on to my face. And then, shambling over the uneven pavement with the street light behind him, came again the tall stooping figure I had been hearing about. We said no word to each other or to him as he passed in the gloom, close enough for us to touch, and it was obvious from his rapt and brooding air and bearing that he was quite unconscious of our presence. We turned and watched him as he went at his laborious shuffle along the pavement and saw him disappear in his swaying overcoat in the direction of the poorer part of the town.

That night in Mr. Jeffreys' house I was haunted by the lined face of the old musician, its sadness, its suffering; again and again at supper, and afterwards in my room, making my preparations for the following day, I pictured the scenes of his life as Mr. Jeffreys had described them to me. His story, told in this way upon that mountain walk, greatly moved me, stirred me to a tenderness and a compassion I did not know to be in my heart. Love and illumination were upon me that night. I wept over the lined face, on my knees I shed my tears into the bosom of Christ at his suffering, and the suffering of the valleys, and the suffering of all the world.

MRS. JEFFREYS

I did not at first think that Mrs. Jeffreys was anything more than a kindly motherly woman zealous for her family and her chapel. I was often in the house alone with her and we frequently ate our midday meal together in the kitchen ; then it was that I found in her, beneath her humour and her wordly concerns, a deep piety and an unexpected tenderness of conscience and a brooding awareness of a divine guidance in her life. She told me a great deal about herself, about her deeply wronged mother and her own hideous childhood and the cruelty and viciousness of her father. One story, recounted over a succession of midday dinners, showed me how superficial my earliest judgement of her had been, and how much richer her experience was, and how much more complex and puzzling, than I in my ignorance and insensitiveness had at first estimated.

Robert had come out of the pit early, she said, because it was Christmas Eve. He was sitting in his shirt-sleeves under the light of the kitchen gas, clean and shining after his bath before the fire, the dinner I had taken out of the oven steaming on the table in front of him. Myra had been put to bed. Gari was only a baby then, he was lying fast asleep by the fire in the clothes basket we used as his cradle.

I had almost finished putting up the Christmas decorations and the holly Robert had cut on his way home from work when I heard footsteps in our back yard. There was a knock at the kitchen door and when I opened it I found one of the neighbours standing in the darkness outside with a message for me. At the sight of my face when I came back into the kitchen and stood under the gas, Robert jumped up from his

meal. "Lowri, what's the matter ?" he asked, alarmed.
"What have you heard ?"

"It's my father," I answered. "Let me sit down. He's
dying. In the *Court*. He wants me. What shall I do ?"

"I didn't know he was back in the valley," Robert said.
"You must go. Shall I come with you ? Or look after the
children ?"

I hurried through the bright streets and the Christmas Eve
crowds without Robert, carrying the baby in the woollen
nursing shawl. Pity for my father, or fear that he would die,
had no part in the agony I felt at hearing that message brought
by our neighbour. I had looked forward eagerly, as I always
did, to Christmas day, to spending the time happily at home
together with my husband and my children, but now that
suddenly was over, I was filled only with bitterness and
resentment, haunted again by the thought of my father's
waywardness and violence. Every memory I had of him was
evil. At one time in childhood, whenever I closed my eyes,
I had before me a horror I could not escape from. It tortured
me. Out for a hill-side picnic with other children during the
summer holidays and wandering off alone I had seen a fight
in a disused railway cutting up on the mountain. Two men
were circling slowly round in the middle of a thick ring of
excited colliers. They were naked to the waist, bare-fisted,
staring hard at each other with their heads down, crimson-
faced, covered with sweat and breathing heavily like animals.
One of the men I recognised as my father. As I watched, looking down in terror from the top of the cutting, I saw him
suddenly rushing in at the other man, shouting out loud ;
he beat his opponent's fists down and struck him a heavy blow
low down on the body, and then a heavier one right in the face.
Even from where I stood I could hear the splashing noise of
his bare knuckles against the man's mouth, and the gasp of
the crowd as he staggered away and went down backwards
on to the ground raising a cloud of dust. At the sight of the
man crouching there kicking and screaming in agony I began
to cry, but before I could move away I saw my father rush up
to him and start to kick him fiercely about the chest and the
face with his heavy pit boots. At that the ring broke up and

the colliers swarmed towards the two fighters shouting. I ran away horrified and before I reached home I was sick. The only memories I had of my father were of his violence and cruelty, and ever since childhood I had hated and feared him. The lives of my mother and me had peace only when he left home, which he did from time to time, sometimes for weeks, sometimes for months on end.

The *Court* was a workmen's lodging house, a big shabby building, one of a row in that old rough part of the town down there by the river where the navvies used to live. The iron-works' railway line ran along in front of it, and on the other side of the line rose a high and rusty cliff of furnace clinker. That part of the town was so dark that in winter the street lamps had to be kept burning day and night. I remember as I made my way along the railway line that Christmas Eve noticing the heavy drizzle drifting about as fine as flour in the light of the gas-lamps.

The front door of the *Court* stood wide open but the whole building was dark and silent. A strong smell of stale air and tobacco and sour clothes came out of the passage. There was no knocker so I shouted into the darkness and waited. This, I thought, my father's rejection and waywardness had brought him to, a deathbed in the squalor and loneliness of a common lodging house. But I felt no pity for him and I found forgiveness hard. Without the shedding of blood, I remembered with shame, Mr. Herbert, there is no forgiveness.

It had been warm carrying the baby all that way in the wrap-around shawl and I was ready to sit down. "Hullo !" I shouted again, banging on the hollow-sounding door. "Is there anybody in ?"

After a time Keefe, the big old man who owned the *Court*, came shuffling slowly along the passage towards me in his shirt-sleeves and slippers, carrying a candle. I knew him by sight, he had been wild, a mountain fighter like my father when he was young, but now he had gone stout and feeble with drink. His big face was inflamed, a mass of red veins, and his eyes were glazed over and very prominent. He looked drunk and dazed, his grey hair on end, as though he had just woken up from a heavy sleep.

"I have been asked to call," I said. "I am told my father is lying ill here. He's Edward Parry."

Keefe swayed above me on the doorstep in those dirty shirt-sleeves, one of his puffy hands trembling as it shielded the candle flame. His heavy drunkard's face looked pear-shaped in the upward light, fattened out into a full neck and a bristling jowl and narrowing across the forehead.

"Ay, he's here," he said in a drowsy indifferent voice. "You're his daughter, are you ?"

I nodded. He turned and shuffled back over the bare flags of the passage and I crossed the doorstep and followed him. As I went I pictured the warmth and comfort of the room I had just left, my own kitchen, clean and brightly lit, with its coloured curtains and cushions and Robert's graining and varnishing on all the woodwork, and with the holly and the paper Christmas decorations everywhere and the fire burning brightly in the fireplace, and I felt a strong wish to hurry with my baby out of the bareness and the dark and the feeling of defilement around me. It was not love or forgiveness that took me along those flagstones, Mr. Herbert, only a wish to do not less for a father than was customary by a daughter in this valley.

At the end of the passage we came to a wooden staircase leading off on the right. "Up there," Keefe said. "There's a turn in the stairs."

I was just going to climb. "Is he very ill ?" I asked him. "What's the matter with him ?"

"You go up and see," he answered. "He's got half his face blown off."

He shuffled away and went on through a door at the end of the passage, taking the candle with him. I was left in total darkness. As I groped my way up the staircase I could feel my legs trembling. At the very top, after the turn, I found the bedroom door in front of me. I fumbled about for the latch and went in.

There was very little light in the room but I could see there were three beds across it, two of them empty. In the one furthest from the window a heavily bandaged figure was lying under a dirty sheet with a khaki greatcoat over it. A candle end stuck in the wrinkles of its own grease stood on the wooden bedpost and threw light down on him. The figure was motionless and very tall, extending the whole length of the bed. Although most of the head and the flesh of the face were under thick bandages I knew it must be my father. His mouth was wide open and his swarthy chin was bare and unshaved ; his eyes, although not entirely covered, were in the shadow of the bandages. I could not tell whether he was asleep or not. I felt my heart shrink away from him in revulsion. I sat down on the tin travelling chest on the side of his bed furthest from the window and waited.

This large shadowy room was an evil place, a sort of attic, the squalor and the stench worse than anything I had expected. Apart from the three beds and a battered chest-of-drawers there was no furniture. Under my boots the gritty boards were bare and the laths showed in large patches in the black walls where the plaster had fallen off. There was no ceiling, and above my head were only rafters, huge and very low, and then the roof-slates. A drying line went in loops across from rafter to rafter with scorched rags of clothing hung on it, and a gridiron, and a blood-stained woollen shirt.

At the furthest end of the room, near the window, a fire was glowing in the grate and the blind man sat crouched beside it in his bowler hat and his long black overcoat. On his lap he held a small sack of cinders and these he fed with his mittened hands in handfuls on to the fire. He was ugly and wretched, a great drunkard, his black-blotched skin hanging slack about his face and down into his bare neck. I always had to overcome feelings of revulsion at the sight of him slouching close to the wall along the street, or sitting begging outside the big market doors, revulsion at his filthiness and at the horror of his large bloodshot eyeballs, staring out always it seemed to me in unseeing hate. He was wearing his high bowler hat and at the sides of his face the thick grey curls hung down in greasy tangles. When the crowds came into town on Saturday nights he sat cross-legged by the open doors of the market with a begging cup beside him and a great braille Bible open on the pavement in front of him ; then, in a raucous, shouting voice, halting at every two or three words, he read his Bible aloud, his sightless eyeballs rolling and prominent in his swaying head and his large red claws creeping over the pages.

When he heard me coming into the room he turned his face to me.

"Woman," he said, in his harsh voice, "what's the weather doing ?"

"It's still raining," I answered. "Drizzling."

He cursed the rain. He wanted to be out in the Christmas Eve crowds reading his Bible and collecting money for drink in his enamel cup.

I sat perspiring on the tin trunk beside my father's bed. The blind man's fire was only a glow, but, carrying the baby, I was wrapped in his woollen shawl, and the window of the attic had been nailed up against the steady rain of grit blowing against it off the clinker tip beyond the railway line outside. I had made up my mind to be patient and to do all expected of me, I sat on quietly in the buzz of the baby's breathing, the raindrops on my lashes sparkling like glass beads in the candle light.

And I remembered in that attic the last time I had seen my father. We were living then, Robert and I, just after we were married, in a lonely cottage up there on the mountain, the one Myra my daughter lives in now. I was alone in the back kitchen one afternoon when I had the sensation of a cold blade suddenly being driven into my body heavily among my bones. Through the window I saw my father, tall and unkempt, coming up the mountain path towards the back of the house. I hadn't seen him for several years and I half believed, and hoped, may God forgive me, that he was dead. But there he was and with him was Hassan, the drunken half-caste who used to be his pub hanger-on, carrying a big fish-basket on his back.

They were already at the garden gate before I roused myself to dash across the kitchen and close the back door. It was an old fashioned door in those days, without a doorknob or a lock, and to open it from the outside you had to put your fingers in, about five feet up, through a round hole the size of half a crown and push up the wooden latch that was on the inside. The door had an iron bolt as well but I knew I would be unable to use it, it was stiff and noisy, and before I could

44

shoot it the footsteps of the two men were sounding on the flagstones of the back-yard outside the kitchen. All I could do was to lean my full weight against the door with my heart pounding painfully. I had not come face to face with my father since my mother's death two years before. She had died of a breast cancer, the disease had spread from a blow he had given her when he was drunk, as he often was. I would have done anything then, or at any other time, anything, to escape the torment and humiliation of his presence.

I heard the two men cross the yard and stand outside the house in silence. They whispered together and then one of them tapped very softly on the door. I did not move, I remained leaning my weight as heavily as I could against the middle of the door. Then two thin dark fingers came in through the round hole and the wooden latch was slowly lifted. The fingers of the half-caste were almost touching the sleeve of my bodice. I stared down at the smooth, strange-coloured finger-nails so close to my shoulder pushing the wooden latch up and then letting it drop back into its socket again with a click. When the fingers were withdrawn there was complete quiet and in the stillness I could hear my heart beating like thunder on the boards at my back. The door started to creak under my weight. What should I do if the two began to force their way in ? I heard my name called softly and quite close. "Lowri, Lowri," my father whispered outside. "Are you there, Lowri ?"

I held my breath. How was it they could not hear the door resounding under the heavy blows of my heart ? My legs began to tremble. I knew I could not stay in this position much longer. Presently I saw the face of the half-caste at the kitchen window peering into the dimness of the room. But at that same moment, before he could see me, the pit hooters sounded in the valley, announcing the end of the day-shift. The two muttered together, cursing as though they were beginning to quarrel, and then they went off across the yard. I shot the bolt and sank on my knees to the floor. Crouching there I wept bitterly, but I did not know why.

I could hear the rats scuffling and squeaking in the attic walls as I sat beside my father's bed. The blind man put his bag of cinders down and groped his way to the window-sill. He took his big Bible off it, opened it across the bed and began to practise his reading. "And in the sixth month," he shouted, using his harsh market voice, his head on his bare neck swaying from side to side, "the angel Gabriel . . . was sent . . . from God . . . unto . . . a city . . . of Galilee . . . named Nazareth . . . to a virgin . . ."

I saw my father stir and pass his tongue over his lips at the sound. "Lowri," he whispered. "Is Lowri there ? Have you come ?"

"Yes," I answered. "Here I am. Can I do anything for you ?"

He rolled his head on the pillow. "I am dying, Lowri," he said. "Dying. Is your husband with you ?"

"No, only Gari. He's my baby. He's asleep in the shawl." Unwillingly I leaned forward towards him with the child. "Here," I said.

"There's somebody else in the room, isn't there," he asked.

The blind man stopped reading and swaying and lifted up his pouched face. He had heard my father's whisper. "You don't expect me to go out in this blasted weather, do you ?" he shouted across the attic. "Blast Christmas Eve, I say. Blast it."

My father sighed. "I am dying, Lowri," he said again. "I have lost blood."

The reading began to echo once more under the slates. My father was lying here because he had tried to poach the river by exploding a stolen shot in the water to kill the fish. These shots are powerful, Mr. Herbert, they are used by the colliers underground to blow out the stubborn coal. The thing had exploded in his face. I was able to understand so much. But his words were hard to follow. Soon his voice began to fail and his mouth fell open again. I thought he was dead. "He shall be great," shouted the blind man, "and . . . shall be . . . called . . . the Son of . . . the Highest . . . and . . . the Lord God . . ."

"'Nhad," I said, getting up frightened, "are you all right ?"

He lay there in silence, not answering, not breathing as far as I could see. Then he began clawing about on the greatcoat along the far edge of the bed, searching for my hand. "Where

46

am I ?" he said suddenly. "Lowri, listen. I want to tell you."

I got up and went round to the other side of the bed with the baby and sat down on the edge. Reluctantly I let my father find my hand. "Shall I stop him reading ?" I asked.

"It was something I heard him reading from his Bible that made me send for you," he said. "He has to do with my forgiveness." He paused again in weakness and passed his dry tongue over his dry lips. He asked me weakly if I remembered Sergeant Probert. I nodded. I did. He was a good man and he had often been kind to my mother and me when we were being molested by my father, and were threatened and in trouble through him. My father hated him, for protecting us, among other things, and also because in spite of his terrible threats of violence the Sergeant was never intimidated by him, he never showed the slightest fear of my father at any time.

He began to confess. He spoke about the time the Sergeant retired, and the night the whole village turned out in respect for the presentation to him. That same night my father went up to Ystrad cemetery on the side of the mountain and found the grave of Probert's son. Not much better than an imbecile that poor Probert boy had been but he had come late in life, an only child, and the old Sergeant had lived for him. When the son died the father had himself carved the gravestone out of white marble, he had taken months over it, it was tall and beautiful. Everybody in the village had seen it, or knew about it. That night of the presentation in the Sergeant's honour my father smashed it to the ground. While the meeting was still being held down in the village he took a stolen sledge-hammer up to the graveyard and battered the marble headstone to pieces.

His words were anguished and excited. He kept rolling his head on the bolster and weeping and asking God to forgive him. Of all the evil he had done why was it this that should disturb him so deeply ? I did not understand. "And his mercy . . . is on them . . . that fear him . . ." came the voice of the blind man from the fireplace behind my back, raucous and discordant. "He hath shown . . . strength . . . with his

47

arm . . . he hath . . . scattered . . . the proud . . . in the . . . imagination . . . of their hearts . . ."

My father went on muttering, asking again and again the forgiveness of God. He wanted me to listen. He let a man die when he could have saved his life. It was Hassan. Hassan the half-caste. He was killed falling from the old viaduct across the valley. He wanted to know if I had heard of it. I was anxious to calm him but there was some great compulsion upon his heart. All I could do was sit beside him on the bed and listen, and feel unwillingly in mine the great bones of his hand.

He and Hassan, he said, used to go down into the railway sidings at night to rob the goods trains. One night they were drunk. It was pitch black and blowing a gale. They left a candle alight in one of the vans while they hid what they had already stolen under the bushes on the river bank, and when they came back to the sidings they found the candle had fallen over into the straw. The inside of the van was ablaze in the wind. They hurried away. The shunters and the signalman up the line saw the fire and came running down the track. My father, with Hassan following him, ran up the bank towards the disused viaduct that went high across the river, it spanned the whole valley high up from mountain to mountain. Hardly any of the parapet stonework was left along its sides by then. The entrances to it were boarded up and barbed-wired and no one was allowed to use it. My father cared nothing for Hassan, all he wanted was to excape. He was not afraid to cross the viaduct even in pitch darkness, drunk, and in a high wind.

He stopped speaking. Behind my back the loud voice of the blind man ran on and on. My father's head rocked on the pillow. I waited but he said nothing. Then he began to breathe more deeply, his breast rising and falling in great agitation under the greatcoat. "Up the bank, Hassan," he whispered in some terrible urgency. "Up the bank. Over the boardings. Chuck your coat over the barbed wire before you climb . . ." I could see he had become delirious. He no longer knew where he was, or who was listening to him, and he wasn't conscious of what he was saying. "Follow me, Hassan," he muttered in the compulsion of some terrible anguish.

"Come on, you blasted fool. What are you afraid of ? Stop screaming my name, damn you, do you want everybody to know who we are ? Why don't you follow me, you half-caste bastard ?" Suddenly he stopped and his voice in a moment trailed off into the silence of exhaustion. "O Christ, O God," he whispered, "what am I saying, what am I saying ?"

"And lo," shouted the blind man, "the . . . angel . . . of the Lord . . . came upon them . . . and the glory . . . of the Lord . . . shone round about them . . . and they . . . were sore afraid . . ."

The candle flickered and went out, leaving the darkness smelling of burning grease. "Lowri," my father whispered, "there is forgiveness, isn't there? For me too there is forgiveness ?"

Even then I had no answer for him. I said nothing, not even a word of comfort. The reading stopped abruptly. The blind man rose from his place by the fire behind me and I heard him shuffle slowly across the gritty floorboards towards the door. Where was there forgiveness for my father if there was none for him in my own heart ? I began to cry.

"Lowri," he whispered again, hardly audible now. "Lowri. I am getting very near the river. Tell me there is forgiveness."

In the darkness I dimly heard the blind man coming across the bare boards and standing behind me, but I took no notice of him as I tried, weeping, to make myself comfort my father. I was too confused, in too much anguish and conflict to feel my usual repulsion at the man's nearness. In his harsh voice he muttered something close behind me that I didn't catch. My father opened his eyes wide, staring over my shoulder, he struggled to rise up in the bed. I put my free arm round him to support him. His weakness was pitiful to see. "Lowri," he said again, desperately, "forgiveness. Your forgiveness. I am talking about your forgiveness." He was hardly able to speak at all now.

"Yes, yes, 'nhad," I said as best I could. "There is forgiveness, for you and for us all. ' Though your sins be as scarlet they shall be as white as snow.' " My heart was full. I wanted nothing but to tell him about the lost sheep, and the missing coin, and the younger son, and the forgiveness we have only to seek. I wept, knowing that this was what he had wanted

49

all the time to hear, and that I, until this last moment, had with-held from him. As I looked down into his face his eyes were wide, fixed and staring from under the bandages into the darkness, and very bright.

I heard the sound of the blind man shuffling off towards the attic door. My father's head rested heavily on my shoulder. The latch of the attic was lifted and I heard someone go down the stairs and leave the house. When everything was silent again my father turned his bandaged face up at me, sighed like a tired child and fell back more heavily against my arm. I knew he was dead. I went on my knees beside him and dropped my face upon the bed, weeping.

Then a voice shouted out loud from the far end of the attic, and my flesh turned to water at the sound of it.

"Lord . . . now lettest . . . thou . . . thy servant . . . depart . . . in peace . . ." the blind man cried out, "according to . . . thy . . . word."

I raised my head, turned, and stared behind me. There he was with the glow of the fire still red upon him in the gloom, he was sitting with his Bible open on the bed before him, his head in its high bowler hat swinging from side to side and his black-mittened fingers still crabbing slowly across the pages.

I do not understand even now what happened, what I heard and felt then. Our Lord said, "I have overcome the World." More than that, Mr. Herbert. The hardness of our hearts too. I know that with the death of my father, I, also, began to hope for forgiveness.

MYRA POWELL

This suffering was a long time ago now, Mr. Herbert, Myra Powell said to me. But nothing is lost. What was in the beginning, is now, and ever shall be. Suffering, I read, passes ; having suffered does not pass.

When I married Gwilym I gave up teaching. I had known Gwilym since we were children, we were in school together and his family belonged to Bethesda like ours. His father owned the timber-yard and Gwilym worked there, he did a bit of everything, from the accounts to driving one of the lorries. He liked this house, where my parents had once lived early in their marriage, it was so healthy up here on the mountain, he said, and he bought it from Uncle Evan, my father's brother. To me it seemed big enough, too big, and old and gloomy. So Gwilym began to alter it. He built those wooden porches round both the outside doors because we are exposed here, and the wind and the rain sweep down on us from the mountain. He put in a new damp-course, and the verandah which is a great protection in summer and winter. He also changed the windows, and cut a completely new one in the kitchen. I first began to like the house myself when I put a clear glass water-jug, filled with white roses, on the new window-sill, and the sun came in and filled up the whole kitchen.

Next door to us, about a hundred yards down the lane, lived my Uncle Evan and his wife, my Auntie Ren. Gwilym was often away from home over-night, driving the lorry, and they were good to me. Uncle Evan brought in my coal and locked me in for the night, he teased me about the alterations Gwilym was making to the house, especially about the bright paint we had on all our woodwork, and our doors, one electric blue and one daffodil yellow. But I was proud of everything Gwilym had done. Only one thing then disturbed my happiness in this house, but it passed.

After four years Ann was born. I was overjoyed when I knew my prayers were to be answered. I hoped very much for a son. Gwilym said he wanted a son too, perhaps to please me. He was a hundred miles away with the timber lorry at the time of Ann's birth, and he did not know he had a daughter until he entered this dining room. From his very first glimpse he was enthralled by her. Very soon he had the telephone brought up here to the house so that he could speak to me about her when he was away. At home he was unwilling to leave the side of her cot. As long as she was small he hurried home here after each trip, he used to drive the lorry right up to the house, up the lane and into the field at the side, and then go straight to her room and gaze at her and put his present at her side— a painting book, say, or a doll with real hair. Anything.

Things she was much too small to play with And until he had nursed her he took very little notice of me. When I told him this his colour went up although I was only laughing at him.

Then, when Ann was three, Alun came. His birth was a hard one, dangerous, the doctor said afterwards, wearisome for me, filled with darkness and misgivings. But I shall never forget the bliss of my first glimpse of him, my son. When my Auntie Ren showed him to me, I had the sensation that the whole bed of my heart suddenly overflowed with joy. I thought I had never seen such a lovely child in all my life. All parents think their own children wonderful, I suppose, but Alun in a day or two had skin like porcelain and his eyes, large and round, were the purest blue, they seemed to be filled always with a lovely radiance. I wanted to have him in bed with me all the time, of course, but I was forbidden ; after the exhaustion of that birth, they said, I was not strong enough for a few days to look after him. And in a short time, to add to his loveliness, his head was covered with a mop of the most beautiful golden curls. But before that happened, his father and I had had our fill of suffering and bitterness.

My auntie had looked after me during my confinement because this house is remote, not easy for my mother to get to from Morlais Road. She was wonderful to me, my aunt, my own mother could not have been kinder, but one thing about her began to puzzle me. I noticed she was very reserved when I spoke to her about Alun's prettiness. I felt hurt at that, that she did not seem to share our joy in what had happened, as I had expected she would. Each time I spoke about the baby she avoided my eyes. I began to be afraid, although I didn't know of what. And at last, one afternoon, I questioned her. Unwillingly and fearfully, she told me. Alun, my beautiful son, was sick. Soon I found out what she meant. His body was incurably deformed.

I couldn't believe it. I had rejoiced so much in his loveliness that her words made me frantic. I half tore off his gown when she brought him in to me in the bedroom, and there I saw the truth of what she had said, I saw his poor deformed body, the beginning of the dwarf's hump on his back, the bulging chest, one of the frail little legs half the length of the other. Under his woollen cap the fontonelle had already closed up.

I wept bitterly. But my chief emotion was not grief, or rebellion even, at first, but a fierce protectiveness. No-one should take this little thing away from me, no-one should pity him, or me, all should accept him, and rejoice in him, as if he were the most beautiful child ever born. I blessed my Uncle Evan when he brought the three half-crowns into the bedroom and put them into my hand. "An old custom now, Myra, *cariad*," he said. "For the child who is king."

Later that day the doctor called. I could see he wished to say something. I thought he did not know my auntie had already told me about Alun. I did not wish to speak to him. Although he was a good man I was stubborn and defiant towards him, I was sure he wanted to talk about Alun's deformity, and to sympathize with me. I asked for no sympathy. My child was still wonderful to me, in my heart I knew there was no virtue or loveliness not in his possession. But the doctor was determined to speak. He asked if Gwilym was at home, and when I said he was he brought him into the bedroom. What he had to say was not at all what I had expected. It was much more terrible. He told us that Alun was not only a cripple. He was also an incurable imbecile.

What a life I led. I neglected Ann, I spent all my time attending to Alun. Ann went unchristened, and although she suffered with her throat I was not interested enough in her needs to have her tonsils removed. All I could think of was my Alun. He used to lie out there on the verandah in his pram, in the sunshine, and when I went to see him his great blue eyes opened wide and looked up at me, they seemed filled with the lovely clear light of love and intelligence. The doctor must be wrong. These could never be the eyes of an imbecile. How I prayed the doctor might be wrong, how I prayed that Alun might grow up straight and sound, and his body be of use in the world, and a burden to no-one. Often I persuaded myself he was becoming more normal, that the dangle of that pitiful little leg was less, and the hump under the pretty nape not so conspicuous. I pestered the doctor and my parents and my uncle and auntie with my questions. "He's getting all

53

right, isn't he, Mam ?" I used to say to my mother whenever she managed to get up here. "He's getting better, isn't he ? Look, he's much stronger than he was this time last week. Look at him."

And then Alun fell ill with pneumonia. I was frantic at the idea of losing him. The doctor tried to reconcile me to it, but his words made me angry and I turned on him. But I must confess he worked hard, he did everything he could to save him. This house is a long way up the mountain but he was here three or four times a day. At last it became more than he could do. Alun had to be taken away to hospital in Ystrad.

I prayed day and night while he was there, not only that he would live but still more that he should grow up to be good and useful. I could not eat or sleep. Hour after hour I lay awake at night waiting for the morning. I can remember how I used to hear the branch of the elder tree in the garden rubbing against the kitchen wall in the wind, and how I used to long for the bedroom curtains to turn blue so that I could get up and prepare to go down to see him in Ystrad.

And Alun recovered. I remember even now my senseless joy when the doctor told me he was out of danger. How I looked forward to having him home again, to carry him about, and to see his great long-lashed eyes looking up with love at me in the kitchen. I seemed to feel my arms full of work even at the thought of it. As soon as he was well enough, I told myself, I would take him out in the red plaid shawl into the garden in the sunlight. I would make him brown and healthy. I would buy him something, many things, to interest him, a clockwork engine, perhaps, that would whistle, or something alive, a bird or a dog. All the time his picture was before me, his curls and his clear blue eyes and the pale blue veins like faded hand-writing, like some message written in a delicate ink under his skin.

But my joy did not last long. Alun never came home from hospital. Within the week he had contracted pneumonia again. I prayed for him as I had done before, as wildly and as constantly, but I felt all the while he would not recover this time. In my heart I knew it, I felt it was all over. And I was filled with bitterness and rebellion at the certainty. Why could not my baby live and grow up ? Why had he to be the condemned ? Could he not live a little, a few years, until he was old enough for school, when all would be altered ? I had seen this happen, and I begged that God might do it for me also. I threatened, may God forgive me for it, sometimes I came near to cursing. But Alun died. I was alone in the house when the hospital phoned me. And I was overwhelmed with rebellion and bitterness and despair. In my heart was chaos, and hatred for God who had deprived and tortured me, I felt all my love for Him was dead for ever.

And then, almost as soon as I had had the message about Alun's death, the phone rang again. I thought it was Gwilym speaking, I thought he had received the message in his father's yard, but it was not. I heard the doctor's voice. I did not want to speak to him, in spite of his kindness and devotion I didn't want to have anything to do with him, or with anyone connected with Alun's illness and death. He sympathised for a moment or two and then, just as I thought he was about to ring off, he asked me something that froze my whole flesh as though it were water. I could not believe my own ears. It was hideous. "Mrs. Powell," he said in his quiet voice. "Would you and your husband consent to our using Alun's eyes ?"

"Alun's eyes !" I shouted. "Alun's eyes ! What do you mean, Alun's eyes ?"

And then, before he could answer, I remembered. I had often heard him speak of taking some part of the eyes of the dead for the use of the blind. And that was what he wanted now. But I could not think of it. Those lovely blue eyes to be taken away, the loveliest part of that poor twisted little body. "No, no," I shouted into the phone. "No, no, you mustn't touch him, you must leave him alone. Do you hear ? Don't you dare to touch him !"

I banged the receiver down. I could feel my heart hammering as though it would burst my chest open. In my anger and agitation I had not heard the lorry stopping in the lane, but now the sweet smell of timber in the room told me Gwilym was home from work and beside me. He knew Alun was dead. Instead of phoning me after his trip he had gone straight to the hospital. I wept against him as though my heart was breaking and it was.

All that evening I could not rest. I told Gwilym what the doctor wanted us to do. And our decision was to be made soon, before midnight. I could not bring myself to consent. Since Alun was gone I cared nothing for the blind. What did it matter to me if they could see or not ? I cared nothing about them, nothing, nothing. Why should I give to others when all that I loved had been taken away from me ?

Gwilym and I took Ann to my uncle and auntie's and left her there and then we went down to Morlais Road. Gwilym persuaded me to do it. But there in my mother's house I acted like someone demented. In the whole world I could see only one thing, that my baby was dead. On the way back we called for Ann and when we reached the house Gwilym left me and went upstairs with her.

I could hear him above me in her room up there playing with her. I knew all the time what he wanted. But he said nothing to persuade me. When Ann was asleep he came downstairs and sat by the fire in silence. His gentleness was crueller than accusations. I wept then the bitterest tears of my life.

As soon as I had made my decision I became calmer. A strange thing happened which at first I rebelled against. Comfort is hard to endure. I began to feel my prayers were answered. The glory of my child's body was alive, and had use and purpose, the blue eyes were not meaningless and without intention. Was I foolish to find healing in this ? I found healing in it and my faith returned.

We have Ann and our second boy now. Having suffered, Mr. Herbert, can never pass.

GARI

There were three people apart from myself living in my lodgings in Morlais Road, namely Mr. Jeffreys, Mrs. Jeffreys and their son Gareth.

Gareth was a colliery surveyor and he seemed to me, in

contrast with his father, a very reserved and even taciturn man. He was a little older than I was, but he seldom spoke to me, and he seemed ready to avoid me always if he could do this without conspicuous rudeness. But one thing he *did* share with his father—a love of reading. Every evening after his bath—he usually came home grimy from work—he used to enter the front room which his parents had set aside for his use and stay there for two or three hours among his books. He seldom went out and he seemed to have very few friends in the valley. I understood from hints and compassionate allusions of his father, that he suffered from a sense of grievance, from some disappointment or frustration, but Mr. Jeffreys did not enlarge to me upon this. I felt ill at ease in Gareth's company, but I heard at last what lay behind his unhappiness.

He suffered, soon after I went to live at Morlais Road, a slight accident underground ; a stone fell out of the roof of a hard-heading on to his foot and forced him to keep it off the floor for nearly a fortnight. During that time I spent part of every day in his room, and little by little he explained his position to me. He was, unlike his father, a dry rather than a dramatic narrator, and he spoke in English. I felt, when he *did* take me into his confidence, that there was something admirable in the candour and completeness of his story. What he had to say, as I have explained, I received from him a little at a time, with many breaks and interruptions, but what I write here is substantially the account he gave me of his misfortunes.

*   *   *

When Nebo and I were together at the university in Dinas, he said, and sharing digs at Mrs. Owen's, no two human beings could have been more unlike in appearance and in every other way than we were. But the funny thing was that many people, at a first acquaintance anyway, attributed my character to Nebo, and his, to some extent at least, to me. Mrs. Owen, our landlady, did. You can see from the photography on the mantelpiece what I looked like then—round-faced and plump, I had black hair, very thick and curly, and hard to keep in order. My clothes, out of regard to the sacrifices my parents were making for me, without being absolutely disreputable, always looked cheap and pretty shabby ; and I spent so much of my time in the college library and out of doors on my geological fieldwork, that my times of returning to my digs were only moderately regular. If my scholarship grant from the Ystrad council was a bit late arriving I failed to pay my monthly board and lodgings on time. The result of all this, the shabby clothes, the untidiness, the irregular hours, the frequent arrears in my rent—the result was that Mrs. Owen looked upon me with dislike and sour disapproval, she thought I was wild and heedless and unreliable. When Nebo was about she ignored me altogether. But him, on the other hand, with his know-all air, and his blarney, and his bald head she treated like someone rich in experience, and of solid judgement. After the way he deflated her boil she came to credit him with skill and wisdom of the very rarest type.

And yet the truth was, Mr. Herbert, that Nebo was so crazy, so idiotic in his behaviour, so completely deficient in even the most elementary common-sense that I sometimes wondered if he wasn't a bit demented. He hadn't the slightest concern for principle or morality ; he was plausible, two-faced, heartless, untruthful and lecherous. You couldn't trust him within a hundred miles of loose cash, and no girl student in the university was safe from him either. No girl student, did I say ? No woman lecturer or professor's wife even, if she happened to be young and the slightest bit attractive.

Of course, nothing I could have said would have convinced Mrs. Owen then that this was true. And why ? Because Nebo, even as a student, had that appearance, when he wanted to put it on, the appearance of a thoughtful and responsible citizen ; his mature look, his suave understanding manner, his man-of-the-world charm, all this inspired respect and confidence wherever he went. In appearance he was tallish, probably six feet in height, and well filled out, without being at all fat, or plump even. His face, I grant, was ugly, but it was very mobile and expressive, it was an actor's face, long and pale and heavily lined, with furrows across the forehead and deep curved incisions down the cheeks. His lips were thick and hideous, wet and dark, like raw liver, his dense eyebrows very blond, white almost, and there were well-filled bags under his eyes. If he knew you were watching him, and if he thought it was worthwhile, he would try to impress you with a bit of thoughtful lip-biting, and head-nodding, and a scowl of heavy meditation. But by far his biggest asset in this farce of pretended earnestness and maturity was his bald head. The bareness of Nebo's scalp was that complete, highly-polished and irremediable nudity that begins in early youth, all the bones and sutures of his skull were plainly visible under the hairless skin and the top of his head was bumpy and irregular, it looked like the battered cranium of a celluloid doll. It was better than the music-hall to hear Nebo talking about this head of his, describing the materials he had rubbed into it to restore the growth, from foreign urine to black pudding. But however much he made me laugh I worried about him. We were both from Ystrad of course, I had known Nebo all my life, and our families were friendly. At first, in Mrs. Owen's, I used to be foolish enough to lie awake at night resenting some sarcasm of his that had wounded me, or agonizing over what I ought to do about the indescribable lunacy of his behaviour. And there, as I lay fretting and worrying, I could hear Nebo snoring away in the other bed, sleeping the sleep of physical satisfaction and conscience undisturbed.

*   *   *

In spite of what I have said, Mr. Herbert, my nature was then, on the whole, pretty placid and equable. But I suffered a mood of deep despondency, I can tell you, when I heard that Nebo was coming to the university and that I was expected to find lodgings for him. The letter I received from his mother asking me to do this I regarded as a kind of augury of disaster, because wherever Nebo went the result was upheaval and confusion. I found lodgings for him—at the other end of the city. But before the year was out I had him, the man I wanted to avoid more than anyone else in the university, sharing rooms with me at Mrs. Owen's lodgings. It came about like this.

I had always regarded Nebo as a sort of lunatic, as I say. Although our parents were friends I had never cared much to have anything to do with him, in school or anywhere else. He was amusing enough, that was one of the most dangerous things about him, but nobody in his senses wanted to be mixed up with the sort of lying and goatish maniac that he had become. We used to go to the same chapel when we were children and one of the very first things I can remember about him was the way he scared the life out of us other children one night on our way to Band of Hope by hoo-hooing about in the chapel graveyard with a white sheet over him. Then another thing. One day when we had passed into the Pencwm grammar school he slipped into the Head's room when there was nobody about, and tried to press a sheet of foolscap on to the jellygraph the Head was preparing our maths exam paper on, so that he would have a copy of the questions beforehand. I always remember the public belting he had for this. As the cane came down on his backside the Head noticed a very peculiar sound, most unusual, and he made Nebo take his trousers down before the whole school to see what was wrong. Outside four or five pairs of football knicks and three blackboard dusters Nebo was wearing the rear half of a pair of home-made cardboard drawers, tied round his waist and thighs with football laces.

Nebo's parents, I ought to say, were in much easier circumstances than mine ; his father was a coal-merchant and his mother owned a row of houses of her own as well. In the end, sick and tired of the complaints from all quarters about Nebo's clowning and destructiveness, they decided to send him away to a public school, somewhere in Gloucestershire I think it was. Within the term he was back home. He had walked all the way. When he reached the house there was nobody in. He was dead tired so he turned their airedale out of the kennel in the garden and went to sleep inside. His father found him there the next morning, still fast asleep and snoring loudly.

He never went back to that school, they wouldn't have him, and some time later we heard he had had a call to the Baptist ministry. But when he was eighteen he eloped with their housemaid in his father's two-seater. People said that the old gentleman refused to have anything more to do with him after that, but whether this was true or not I don't know, because by this time I was in college. I ought to explain, though, that the elopement wasn't much of a success, because before Nebo had got out of the valley he had driven the car into a butcher shop through the plate-glass window.

What I do know is that about this time he left home and was in lodgings at the other end of the valley. I found this out when I met him in Ystrad one day during the summer vac. We went to have a couple of games of billiards together and I just couldn't pot the balls for laughing. He had got a job selling paper doyleys from door to door. There wasn't much demand for this sort of thing in Ystrad then and he was short of cash. But I couldn't believe this, Mr. Herbert, he was dressed beautifully, as usual, he smoked the most expensive cigarettes one after the other and he wouldn't let my pay for our billiards. He told me he was so hungry, often, he would go down to his mother's house when she and his father were out in chapel and stretch his arm in through the pantry window for a long swig of milk or a slice out of the cake-tin. But his mother was worried to death over him, naturally, he was an only child and he had the name of having been a delicate baby. She used to go up to his lodgings to see how he was getting on. He said he had a card on the wall, hung up ready for her, with "What is home without a mother?" printed on it. She used to cry, poor thing, at his descriptions of his meals—a Welshcake and a cup of water for breakfast and a bread faggot for his Sunday dinner.

I lost touch with him about this time, as I say, because I was away from the valley in college, but it seems *he* left the area too about then and I heard occasionally that he had been seen in various parts of the country by Ystrad people who knew him—sleeping in a booky's car on Epsom Downs, in a song and dance act on the variety stage in Manchester, working as a wine-waiter in a West End Hotel, and so on. I heard too that after some unpleasantness over a cheque he had gone abroad.

And then, towards the end of my third year in college, I had news of him again in my weekly letter from my mother. "Who do you think is back in Ystrad ? Alcwyn Davies ! (Alcwyn was

Nebo's real name). He's been all over the world, they say. Looking very well, but old, and as bald as a badger. There's improved he has, you wouldn't know him, so attentive and sensible. Quite settled down. He was in chapel last Sunday night with his mother and they asked him to say a few words in second meeting. He spoke lovely. He said how everything he had learnt in the Sunday school and the Band of Hope had kept him on the right lines during his travels and brought him to what he was now. You ought to have heard the ' Amens ' ! His poor mother was a proud woman, I can tell you. Tears of course . . ."

The only things I could remember Nebo taking real interest in in the Band of Hope were his stink-bombs and his itching dust and his sneezing powders, he used to nearly drive the poor women in charge of the meetings mad with his cheek and clowning. But I felt perhaps it was unkind to recall things like that after reading my mother's words. Anyway, before long I had another letter, from Nebo's mother this time, asking me if I could find rooms near me in Dinas for Alcwyn, as he had been accepted at the medical school and was coming up to the university the following term. My heart sank at this, as I said before, I was filled with gloomy forebodings, but I did manage to get a place for him to lodge, although, of course, not anywhere near me.

I didn't meet him at all during the long vacation because he had gone to some medical cram school in London, but when he came up to the university the following term I used to see him fairly often in the common room, with the card-playing gang usually, but I was always in a hurry when we met. It was deadly to let Nebo work on you, Mr. Herbert. He would get you laughing describing some fantastic adventure that was supposed to have happened to him, and the next thing you knew you had said goodbye to a ten bob note.

And then one night, just when I was going to have my supper, I heard a knock at the front door of my digs and who should be there but Nebo. I had felt all the time, somehow, that this was going to happen. He came into my room and began looking round and admiring the place in a way I didn't like at all. He was wearing lovely suede shoes that night, I remember, brogues, almost yellow in colour, and a smart dark brown suit with knife-pleated trousers. Nebo always managed to have something in his clothes a bit different from the ordinary and that time it was a sort of double-breasted waistcoat with lapels, it had a sort of collar to it. He also wore a brown and white spotted bow-tie. I often felt dislike and uneasiness in his presence, and resentment, too, at the patronizing and insulting way he would sometimes talk to me, but I had to admit that night that in spite of his spongy lips and his pouched-up eyes he did look impressive ; with the fireplace gaslight falling on his face and his pink head, he did have that distinguished air that's enough to inspire respect and confidence in so many people.

But there was another thing I didn't like about him that evening and that was his affability. Except when he wanted something he didn't go out of his way to be pleasant to me. When we met, knowing the state of my finances, he was in-different to me and often, as I say, contemptuous and offensive. That evening he started trying to make me laugh but I was wary and suspicious and I refused to respond. I wondered what he was after, and at last it came out. He had been turned out of the digs I had found for him. The opera company was in Dinas that week and Nebo, so he claimed, had got a job with them for a few of their performances, he was the silent Negro headsman in "Turandot." He wanted to do the part properly, he said, so he had blackened himself all over, not only his face and hands, but when he went to get the stuff off after the show he couldn't, he had to go to bed with it on, and the landlady had thrown him out because of the mess he had made on the sheets. Did I happen to know any other place where he could stay ?

I felt sure all this about Turandot was only a lot of lies. Most likely he hadn't paid the rent. I said no, impatiently, I didn't know of a place ; and I thought I was going to get rid of him because he gave up trying to humour me and yawned and wiped his hands over his face with boredom. But just then Mrs. Owen had to come in with my supper. I could see in a flash from the sort of look she gave him that if he started talking I was finished. He was sitting on the sofa when she came in but he rose and cleared a chair out of her way so that she could put the tray of crockery on the sideboard. I cursed my luck but I had to introduce them, and then Nebo turned on his flood of blarney. First he agreed with her about the changeable weather we were having and it seemed to me in no time they were in absolute and complete accord no matter what subject they began talking about.

Then Nebo started to be concerned about Mrs. Owen's health. At that time she had a big ugly boil on the side of her face, just in front of her ear, which, she soon began to tell Nebo, her doctor didn't seem able to cure at all. A look of interest and sympathy came over his face. He was practically a qualified physician and surgeon, he said, he wondered if he might have her permission to examine it. He was very diffident and hesitant saying this, as though it would be a great honour if she were willing. He touched her very respectfully, reluctantly, almost, the clown, he put her to sit by the fireplace with her head on one side under the gaslight. And then he began his examination.

I have never before or since seen anything like what followed, or heard such utter guff spoken with so much absolute seriousness—solemnity, I ought to say. But I must say at the same time that I was, as usual, half mesmerised myself; I found myself succumbing to some extent to the idiotic and elaborate clowning. Nebo turned his sleeves back—heaven knows what for—and first delicately prodded the skin round the boil with his fingers. Mrs. Owen seemed to have gone off into some sort of trance, she didn't even wince. He moved her ear up and down very slowly, asking her in a soothing, purring sort of voice if this was giving her pain. She didn't answer. She sat absolutely motionless under the light with her lids down. He got her, still in her trance, to cross her legs and began tapping her knees with a dessert spoon. After a few minutes of this he apologized for not having his stethoscope with him and again, very respectfully, asking her permission, he knelt down by her side and pressed his ear against her chest. "Breathe deeply, please," he said. A half-smile of daft happiness appeared on her face.

Then he returned to the boil. He put his heavily rimmed

glasses on and hovered over it without a word, he peered at it from all angles, frowning, screwing up the big jube of his face, biting his lips and nodding his bald bulgy head as though the big light had at last started breaking before him.

Then he spoke. At that time he had hardly been in the medical school long enough to have tasted mother's milk in his tea, but to hear him jawing you could think his whole life had been spent in the study of boils, especially boils on the cheeks of middle-aged women just in front of the ear. I was used to him but, as I say, I was a bit impressed myself. He wasn't modest or diffident any more. He seemed to blaze with certainty and an urgent sense of mission. He got Mrs. Owen round out of her sock and told her he knew exactly what ought to be done. He was confident he could cure that boil in no time at all. No doubt her doctor was well enough but the trouble with the ordinary practitioner was that he was old-fashioned, he very soon lost touch with the latest researches of medical science. He, now, would prescribe a daily oil-massage. A little painful at first, perhaps, but nothing really. In a few days, he could guarantee, the boil would be no more than a memory.

Mrs. Owen was a very vain and good-looking woman and this big, unsightly boil throbbing on her face must have worried her a good bit. She listened hard and took in everything Nebo said. The next thing I understood was that they were arranging for him to apply the treatment himself. And then, of course, the question of his digs came up. He was just leaving his present lodgings because the fleas were infesting the beds— well, that's what he hinted. Nebo knew exactly, Mr. Herbert, when the Queen of Spain has no legs. He pretended he was too squeamish to lay his tongue to a coarse word like ' fleas ' when speaking to a lady of Mrs. Owen's kidney. What he said, grinning, was that every night he was conscious of being only one of a very large number of occupants of his bed. Anyway, the clear solution was for him to come and stay at Mrs. Owen's, at any rate until the treatment was completed, and the very next night he was there, he and I had a single bed each in my own room.

When Mrs. Owen had gone back to her kitchen that night

65

I felt a very powerful sensation of anger against Nebo. I really was furious at having been completely ignored like this, at not having been consulted at all as to whether I would have Nebo as a co-digger. In my temper I said, "Now look here, Nebo, I'm not so stuck on this Mrs. Owen, but she can cook, she keeps this place comfortable and she doesn't try to rook me. So if you're coming here, no funny business, mind."

When I said that Nebo looked shocked and hurt as though I had wounded him deeply. He couldn't understand what I was talking about. "Funny business ? What do you mean ' funny business,' Gari ?" he said, absolutely bewildered. Well, to see him sitting there on the sofa fingering his beautiful clustery cufflinks and looking so innocent and hurt, I couldn't help myself, I had to grin at the absolute cheek and perfection of his act. And at that *he* grinned too and before we had finished supper, although my resentment and foreboding hadn't vanished by a long way, I was coughing and swallowing my food the wrong way, laughing at the fantastic craziness of his experiences.

That was how I came to have the biggest liar and the most debauched and plausible lunatic in the university as my co-digger.

* * *

The rest of the term passed with Nebo becoming more and more moody and unpredictable. He seemed, for a few weeks at least at the beginning, to have found a real interest in medicine, he was lively and buoyant all the time, and this, I felt, I ought not to hinder in any way. Many a night when he had come home very late, after I had gone to bed, he moithered me out of my warm blankets with his blarney and used me for elaborate physiological examination ; he stood me naked and shivering on our bedroom oilcloth and passed his icy hands over me, he shook his head and looked serious when he said he couldn't find anywhere in my anatomy some process or other normal in the human frame. He was so plausible I often found myself the next day worrying over his words,

66

fingering myself on the quiet, wondering if there was really some truth in what he had been telling me the night before.

And by some miracle or other Mrs. Owen's boil was cured. He used to work on it for ages every day, very enthusiastic he seemed to be, massaging the inflamed lump lower and lower on her face until he had moved it into the soft flesh below the angle of the jaw. Here he lanced it and in a short time there was no trace of the thing to be seen, nothing at all except a small hidden scar.

There were two results of this really staggering cure. From then Mrs. Owen's attitude to Nebo was almost idolatrous, she treated him as though he possessed some special, almost supernatural, skill and wisdom. And to Nebo himself the cure gave a very unhealthy interest in boils and pustules as such, for a few weeks nobody in the university with a few unsqueezed pimples could feel safe from Nebo's healing zeal.

But none of this enthusiasm lasted. He began spending a lot of time in an expensive badminton club in the city, where the people, I heard, called him Dr. Bowen-Davies. It was here, I suppose, he met the girl he claimed to have run away with. I don't know. Lying had become to Nebo by then something more than a way of impressing strangers, or amusing his friends, or avoiding the consequences of some idiocy ; it had evolved into a sort of grace, a refinement of existence, an activity of the spirit, as they say, to be indulged in entirely for its own sake without regard to purpose or advantage.

I remember one instance of this very well. It happened after I had spent a day on the Bryngwyns carrying out a geological survey. I was tired and hungry when I got back to digs that night and I dare say I looked even rougher than usual, more crumpled and wind-blown. Presently, almost as soon as Mrs. Owen had brought supper in, Nebo appeared. He was wearing a black tie and a wide crepe band round his arm. I was startled at this and I heard Mrs. Owen asking him what had happened. Very awed and sympathetic she sounded too. Nebo lifted his hand and shook his head, as though the subject was too painful for him to talk about. "My father," he murmured huskily, like somebody absolutely shattered

67

with grief. "Dead. Telegram. Drowned at sea. Off Bloody Foreland. Body lost."

I was stunned. I couldn't believe my ears. When I heard this absolutely idiotic and gratuitous lying I just stared, I couldn't say anything at all. But when Mrs. Owen had gone out I said, "What the devil did you say that for, Nebo ?"

"Say what, Gari ?" he asked me. His blond eyebrows were still knitted after the act he had put on for Mrs. Owen and he looked hurt as well at my attack.

"Say your father was dead, you fool," I answered, exasperated.

"Well he is, isn't he ?" he asked me cheerfully, and his big mouth went into a wide grin inside the brackets on his cheeks.

"Yes," I said, "he is. But he died three years ago. And he wasn't drowned, anyway. Off Bloody Foreland, my eye."

"Gari," he said, coming over to me and dropping his big face down almost on top of mine, "Gari," he said, "have you shaved today ? You ought to stand much nearer to the razor, you know. Honestly, I'm worried about you, Gari. All you care about is giving your Mam the satisfaction of seeing BSc., Hons, after your name. Nothing else matters at all. Look at you now in that suit, you're about as glamorous as a nun's umbrella." He caught sight of a letter on the mantlepiece behind me and reached over my shoulder for it.

"Ah," he said, turning away, "from the old lady herself, God bless her, the one and only Emily Sarah Bowen Davies."

He held the letter in front of him for some time, staring at it. Then he opened it and took out a cheque which he placed very carefully in his pigskin wallet. The letter itself he pressed passionately again and again to his lips and then—I say this with shame, Mr. Herbert, even when I am speaking about Nebo Davies—and then he tore it up and threw it unread into the fire.

"Don't get up in the bows, Gari," he said to me, seeing me scowling at him, I suppose, "and don't start pouting at what I tell you. Try to see yourself objectively, will you? That tie you've got on now. Honestly, is it home-made?" He ragged me like this for a time, he was in an expansive sort of mood, and after supper we sat talking pleasantly enough by the fire, going

68

over the people we knew in the valley—the chapel deacons, the neighbours, the grammar school masters and so on. He seemed untroubled that night, quite at ease, he wanted to smoke a pipe for a change and to do this in comfort he had to take his bottom teeth out and put them in his trousers pocket.

But he was less and less often so pleasant as the term went on. Sometimes he came downstairs to breakfast sullen and baggy-eyed and morose, and ate his porridge in silence. If I made a remark he snapped some obscenity back at me, or said something insulting, or just twitched irritably and didn't answer at all. And then, the week before his yearly exams, he began to appear with his right arm heavily bandaged and carried in a sling across his chest. He had picked up an infection from one of his patients, he told Mrs. Owen, although of course he hadn't started to walk the wards then. He couldn't sit his examination because he was unable to write. After the summer vacation I heard that Nebo was not to return to the medical school.

But that was not the end of his studies, unfortunately. By some clever piece of manoeuvring, probably on his mother's part I should think, he was allowed to begin his college career all over again the following term, this time as an arts student. But he didn't tell Mrs. Owen this because he wanted to stay out all hours drinking and playing poker when she thought he was busy at the hospital.

I ought to say, Mr. Herbert, that our landlady had never once to wait even a day for her money for Nebo's board and lodging because every week a cheque was sent directly to her from Mrs. Bowen Davies, and Nebo never had any chance at all of laying his hands on it.

*   *   *

During my honours year I saw very little of Nebo. What he had said in his jeering way about my wishing to please my parents was true and I did work very hard so that I would leave college with a good degree. At that time this was more important to me than anything else. I got gradually more used to Nebo's moods and I learnt to ignore his insults and his strange behaviour. I certainly did not allow myself to worry so much about him as I had done when he first came to dig with me.

When Nebo did his studying, if he did any, I don't know. Whenever I spent a night at work in our lodgings, which was quite often that year, he always had some appointment or other and had to go out. But one evening towards the end of term, when I got my books out of the cupboard after tea, I was surprised to see Nebo doing the same. He seemed to read seriously and during a break for a smoke I asked him how he was getting on with his course. He bulged his lips out, narrowed his eyes and made a fast cutting sweep in front of his face with the edge of his hand, which I took to mean that his work had been successful, and satisfactory to himself. And then his expression changed suddenly. "That reminds me, Gari," he said, with his thoughtful scowl, "I've got to turn up something. I heard somebody mentioning a book in our course this morning that I haven't read at all. In fact I've never even heard of it. And our exam starts in two days' time. 'A Woman of Kilmer Kyness.' That's it. Have you ever come across it?"

I said no, I hadn't, but then I knew very little about things like that. What was it, a poem, a play, a novel, or what?

Nebo said that was part of the difficulty, he didn't know. He had overheard a group of men of his year talking about it that morning but he was too busy at the piano at the time to ask about it.

With that he got up and fetched the comprehensive syllabus of university courses. We hunted up the section dealing with his faculty but 'The Woman of Kilmer Kyness' did not appear there at all, not in the lists for general or detailed study. Twice or three times we went through those lists—Chaucer's ' Prologue and Three Tales ' ; Shakespearean Comedies ; Milton's ' Comus ' ; ' The Rape of the Lock and other Poems '; Six Jacobean Plays ; ' The Lyrical Ballads ' ; Longer Narrative Poems ; but we could find no trace of the mysterious title. I thought this was very strange because Nebo had a mind like a magnet, a rather weak one no doubt, that could and did pick up small unimportant objects that crossed its path, and picked them up whole. At last he got tired of searching and began making jokes, but I could see he was puzzled too. He couldn't start work again, he said, without finding out about 'The Woman,' so he put his coat on and went up to Tonza Griffiths's to ask him about her. Tonza was a student living a few hundred yards up the road who was doing the same course as Nebo. He was an expert poker player, but he was debarred now from the students' hall for dropping a typewriter from an upstairs window into the lily-pond. From what I knew of him I wouldn't have guessed Nebo could have made reference very profitably to him on academic matters.

When Nebo had gone I went back to my work and I had soon forgotten all about his problem ; but the next morning, at breakfast time, he started talking about the book again. The funny thing was, he said, that when he asked Tonza about 'The Woman of Kilmer Kyness' he found Tonza had never heard of her either. To me this did not seem remarkable since Tonza seldom read any printed matter apart from the sporting pages of the newspapers. But Nebo appeared puzzled, almost obsessed by this title, and he told me he was determined to get to the bottom of the mystery.

What the result of his enquiries was I never found out because that night he didn't come back to digs at all. The next day, when I was out at the library, he called in to see Mrs. Owen. He apologised for his absence that night before and said he would be away from the lodgings indefinitely now between then and the end of term, because of pressure of work at the hospital. He had quite a chat with her apparently, blarneying as usual and trying to make her laugh. He had just come from examining a male patient, he said, an old-fashioned looking deaconish type of man dressed all in black, black suit, black boots, black hat, black tie—but when the old chap stripped off for Nebo to examine him—what a surprise !—all his underclothes were bright scarlet—socks, vest and drawers, all Welsh flannel and red as a pillar box ! That was Nebo all over, Mr. Herbert, always the tall story, the lies, the plausible yarn.

Mrs. Owen reported all this to me, very pleased and flattered. I listened to her with great uneasiness and all my old fears and worries returned. A sort of gloomy foreboding settled on my mind just when, because my examinations were approaching, I wanted to be as free as possible from all anxiety. What was happening, I wondered, where was Nebo spending his time, what was the reason for his absences, what deceit, or worse, was behind his lies and his disappearances ? All my latent dislike of his insincerity and hypocrisy returned.

For a whole week I never saw him at all. And then, one evening, the day before I was to sit my first exam paper, something happened to bring us into contact with each other again.

I had worked very hard all that term, as I said, and towards the end of it I began to feel physically the effects of too little sleep and too much application to books and to study. I was sitting that evening in my digs with a heavy volume dealing with the western coalfield on my lap, and when I opened my eyes and glanced sideways from it my head began to swim, I was puzzled to find the carpet only about eighteen inches from my eyes. I couldn't remember falling at all and I had not hurt myself, but I thought this sort of faint meant it was time I shut my books for an hour and took a stroll through the gardens opposite our lodgings—which was, at that time of the year, the length of my chain.

It was a lovely June evening, the sky blue and the air warm and still, but my body seemed somehow inflated, and my mind was airy and weightless, I felt as though I was suffering pretty badly from the weakness of hunger although I did not want food. And through this sort of mental blankness I could hear snatches of the paragraphs I had been learning by heart buzzing about, classifications and locations of strata and so on, and every now and then the words of Nebo's mysterious title, ' The Woman of Kilmer Kyness, The Woman of Kilmer Kyness.' I crossed the road feeling pretty unsteady and went into the park, but before I had gone many paces beyond the gates a young woman got up from her seat and began speaking to me.

"Excuse me, please," she said. "I was sitting here and I saw you leave your house. I wonder if you know Mr. Bowen-Davies."

I was in such a dizzy state that I found it hard to realize the

72

girl was actually speaking to me, and I'm afraid I didn't answer her. For one thing, I hadn't often spoken to such an attractive girl before. Of course, I knew a fair number of women in college, but they all seemed to wear glasses and to smell, most of them, of the more penetrating chemicals. This girl was absolutely different, she was slim and tall and extremely pretty. What she was wearing I couldn't remember afterwards but I knew she had auburnish curls and a sort of emerald tamoshanter. Her eyes looked green to me and I particularly noticed her skin, very fine-textured, and pallid. But my mind was only slowly recovering from its airiness and blankness, I was quite unable to take in details, and what I bore away from my meeting with this girl was only a general impression, prettiness and elegance, and lilac perfume, and a low resonant voice and a sense of refinement.

I said nothing in reply to the girl at first, as I explained, and I saw her colour slightly. I made an effort of will and memory and answered yes, I did know Bowen-Davies.

"I wonder if he still lives in the same place," she asked.

I assured her he still had rooms in the house. She took her net-gloved hand out of her coat pocket and held out a letter towards me. "In that case," she said, "I wonder if you would be so good. Would you please hand him this note?" She smiled, said, "Thank you. Goodnight," and hurried away.

I sat down on the park bench with the letter in my hand and tried to think. What had I undertaken to do? I didn't know where on earth Nebo was. Should I keep the letter until he turned up? Or hand it to Mrs. Owen in case he called at the house when I was out? What if it was urgent? Ought I to spend some of my precious time trying to find him?

I decided I would do this. I would go to Tonza's first. But I was puzzled and disturbed. Who was the girl I had spoken to? Why had she had anything at all to do with a flag like Nebo? The old refrain began to dance again through my mind, 'The Woman of Kilmer Kyness, The Woman of Kilmer Kyness.' And then, suddenly, this sensation of dizziness and uncertainty vanished; like a thunderbolt came the realization that the unknown girl was going to have a baby.

*   *   *

73

Tonza's lodgings were not very far away from ours. When I opened the door of his room I saw Nebo at once, standing in his shirt-sleeves in the middle of the room with his back to me. There were three others present, Tonza himself, Inky Greening and Gunner. They were all smoking and the small room was thick with tobacco fumes. Tonza was squatting on the hearth-rug stripped to the waist examining his shirt and jabbering about his greyhound, Roxy. Gunner sat at a side-table near the window working at a piece of translation. Nebo had Inky Greening sitting on a chair in front of him swathed in the red plush tablecloth and he was doing something to his hair.

I had no idea what to say to Nebo when I should find him, so I replied to the greetings and sat down hoping to think up some plan or other. To be with Nebo and his friends when they weren't silent over a card game I always found bewildering. It was like bedlam. Every one of them always seemed to be concerned only with working out his own pattern of talk and behaviour, and these patterns had no connection at all with each other as far as one could see. Their talk was a mad and baffling mixture of jokes, obscenities, private references and wild interjections, it was endless, but idiotically disjointed, there was no shape or coherence to it and I found it very hard to put up with. I never attempted to join in and I sat now near the door wondering how I could tell Nebo about the letter in my pocket. Was it confidential ? Would he be angry if I explained before his friends how it had come into my hands ? I had no experience at all of any sort of intrigue which would help me to determine how I should carry out my under-taking.

Nebo seemed in hight spirits. He was shaving the top of Inky Greening's head with an open razor. Inky, he explained to me, had begun to lose his hair at the crown, he was having four square inches of scalp shaved every day by Nebo to make the hair grow again. Inky, while being shaved, was guying their coming examinations in a string of mock questions. Gunner—I never knew what his real name was—Gunner, as I say, was surrounded with dictionaries, translating a piece of German prose, and smoking, and eating a banana dipped in a pot of black-currant jam. Tonza, on the mat, went through the examination of his shirt like a chattering monkey.

"Well here's old Gari," Nebo shouted to them when I went in, "old small-sentence Jeffreys. How's things, Gari ? You don't look too gay, *mon ami*. Rather down *danz la boosh*, as we say in Paris and the upper Ystrad valley." (He was still wearing the silver-barred tie of the medical school, I noticed.) "You know Tonza, don't you, Gari ? And Gunner ? And Inky here under this barber's sheet ? Listen, all. Shut up with that German, Gunner, you're like a ha'penny book. Now listen, I've seen our Gari growing, we were kids in Ystrad, brought up together on the breast of the Sunday school. Honestly, we used to suck the same orange. Listen to what I was told ; when Gari came to the university first—this is what I heard, I don't know if it's true of course—when he came here first he was a real Shoni, he used to take his cap off to go into the college bogs because it was all marble inside. I don't know if that's true mind, as I say, but one thing I can vouch for—he's got tougher since. Honestly, now he's no better than one of the wicked, his whole life is one long stagger from Boar's Head to whore's bed . . ."

Nebo could keep this sort of idiotic banter up indefinitely, so I just sat there by the door feeling rather numb again, and not saying anything. If I had been more wide-awake I think perhaps the undercurrent of sneering in Nebo's words would have hurt me, but what attention I was capable of in that chatter and thick tobacco smoke I gave to the problem of passing the letter over to Nebo.

"Gari's mother," Nebo went on, wiping the razor, "used to buy her coal from the firm of D. Bowen Davies and Son, Ystrad Valley. That's the old man and me. Wonderful coal my old man used to sell ; you could do everything with it except burn it. Keep still, Inky, you crawn, mind this razor or I'll be through to your brains. Where do you think I've been since I saw you last, Gari? Paris! *Ah, ma chérie, do you remember the moon rising and a leaf afloat on the river ?* I spent two hundred quid in less than a fortnight. Never mind, I've got a motor-bike out of it. I lost the train from Paddington and I bought it to get back here before tomorrow. A Super. Twelve horse-power. Ninety-five miles per hour unpaced. Honestly, you must let me give you a ride, Gari. Listen, boys, I haven't told you this before. Do you know what happened when I was in Paris ? My landlady was battered to death one night when I was where I shouldn't have been. Political thugs. Honestly. A polish countess she was, four feet high and covered with tattoo. And talk about drink ! I've seen her before breakfast pouring a whole bottle of hot sauce down her throat when she happened to be short of gin. She loved it. Oh, and one night suppertime I was shaking the sauce bottle before pouring it out on my meat and the cork flew out. The stuff shot up into the air like a fountain and on the way down it landed splash on the top of my bald pate. And honestly, if I was to drop down dead here, do you know what she did ? She climbed up on the rung of my chair and licked it all off, in a minute or two the top of my nut was as clean as if I had washed it."

"Here's a dead certain question," Inky interrupted. "Absolute certainty ! Listen ! Quote. ' Oh that this too, too solid flesh would melt.' Discuss uses for liquid Hamlet. What do you think of that for a likely ?"

Nebo ignored him. "What was I talking about ? Your humour gets right up my nose, Inky."

"That the national pastime of Wales," Inky continued, "is nosepicking. Discuss this from your knowledge of the life and institutions of the country."

"How does this strike you for Rilke, boys ?" Gunner asked, laying down his banana. He swept his hair back with one hand like an actor and held the manuscript well out before him with the other. "And his scented locks were spread out over the young knight's neck like the hair of a woman."

"*Honi soit qui mal y woollen pants*," said Inky. "Give context of above, and comment upon it from . . ."

"Talking about landladies," said Nebo, "how's Owen, Gari ? God bless her. Honestly, since I cured her carbuncle she thinks the sun shines out of me."

"Our landlady," Tonza said getting up and putting his shirt on, "old Ma Hartland, she's a witch if ever there was one. I wonder which of us is *really* going to get married. That's the

76

point. There's not much time left now. But if she says it—there's sure to be something in the wind."

"She was in here just before you came, Gari," Nebo said to me. "She can read the tea cups and the cards. She said she wouldn't mention any names but one of us—she could touch him with a short stick—was going to get married in a few days' time. And she's always dead right. Isn't she, Tonza?"

"Discuss either the action of music on steam," said Inky, "or the Thomist belief that Welsh goats breathe through their ears."

"She's dead right," said Tonza. "Always. Last week me and Gunner enter our greyhound in a dizzy track up there in Pencwm. You never saw such a hole. They'd got a bike turned upside-down to wind the hare on and the track's so bumpy the rabbit-skin takes a flying leap six feet into the air every few yards. Ma Hartland tells us it's in the cards our Roxy's bound to win, but there are some good dogs against him, and in spite of her we don't think he will. So we lay heavy bets on another dog, everything we have, and to make sure we give our Roxy thirteen pies and a bucket of water. And even then the old witch is too much for us. Roxy gets home with three lengths to spare and me and Gunner are broke ever since."

"Who or what are the following," said Inky, "Faithful Teat, Rosie Haas, the Woman of Kilmer Kyness . . ."

In the smoke of that small room I could feel my light-headedness beginning to return. I saw Inky standing up before the mirror and I watched him in a confused way combing his dark crinkly mop back over the shaved spot at the top of his head. Nebo looked at his watch. I heard him saying he had promised to examine the fish-and-chip woman down the road who was complaining her rupture came down when she ate fresh bread. I got up to go with him but before I could open the door I felt myself becoming dizzy and I sat down again.

When I came to, the first thing I set eyes on was Nebo's bald head. He was bending over me, and close to my face was the top of his hairless scalp with the shape of a large depression in it, as though all the hair roots had once been embedded in a sort of pink matrix. I was lying in the little tiled area in front of Ma Hartland's house, my head on Tonza's knees, while

Inky knelt by my side with a glass of water in his hand. When I was on my feet again they arranged that I should go back to my lodgings on the pillion of Nebo's new bike, a rush through the fresh air would revive me completely, they said. I welcomed this because it would give me a chance to be alone with Nebo and to hand him the letter, so I agreed.

Nebo went round the corner into the lane to fetch his machine and in a few minutes we were away. What a bike it was, huge and heavy, all scarlet and glittering with two large cylinders and long handlebars that came back to meet you. It went down the street with a deafening roar but we had only just taken the first corner when the engine sputtered and came to a standstill. This was my chance, I thought. As we stood side by side on the kerb examining the machine I handed Nebo the letter, explaining how it had come into my hands.

He looked at it a moment, grinned, said, "Oh glory," and put it carefully in his pocket.

"Thank you, Gari," he went on. "I'm afraid our trip is *wedi popi*, boy. I'll give you a ride some other time, shall I? Honestly, I don't know what's gone wrong. She came down from London today like a two-year-old. Shall I come back to Owen's with you? I must wheel the old bus back to the garage first..."

I told him not to bother. I had done what I set out to do and I was satisfied now. I walked back to my lodgings alone and went upstairs to the bedroom. I did not undress but lay down on the bed in my clothes. I meant to get up in an hour's time and go back to my books. But I fell fast asleep, Mr. Herbert, and when I woke up it was early morning.

*　　　*　　　*

It was then I was taken for the ride Nebo had promised me.

I slept heavily when I lay down on the bed, as I say, but some time after midnight I woke up. Work was out of the question at that time of night so I took off my clothes and went into bed. But I couldn't sleep, I tossed about thinking of the exam I would have to sit that afternoon. I must have dozed off for a time because the next thing I remember was, as I say, that it was beginning to get light.

I rose and went downstairs to start some revision, feeling pretty common. I took some books out of the cupboard and drew back the curtains and opened the window a bit. I had the surprise of my life. Standing on the kerb outside the house was Nebo. He was dressed in a complete motoring get-up—mackintosh suit, leather helmet, goggles and gauntlet gloves. When he saw me he came in through the gate grinning, the ends of his lips disappearing into the sides of his helmet. I slid the window up a bit further and leaned out. He had only just arrived he said, how lucky, just when I opened the curtains. Yes, he had the bike, it was there at the corner. Could I hand him that book on the mantelpiece, the green one, ' Six Jacobean Plays ' ? He was being examined in it that afternoon. Did I feel like a spin now ? Come on. Do me good. The morning was balmy. I didn't want a coat or anything. Just round the block . . .

I had only my thin pyjamas on and a pair of soft slippers, but I thought a short ride round the gardens might freshen me up and give me an appetite for the two or three hours work I meant to do before breakfast. This, Mr. Herbert, was the greatest mistake I could have made, and all my disappointments have arisen from it. It seems to me now impossible that, knowing Nebo as I did, I should yet agree to do this unbelievably foolish thing. But there, I did it.

I slipped out through the window and hurried with Nebo along the pavement to the corner where he had left that dreadful scarlet motor-bike. It was only a little past daybreak then and there was not a soul to be seen, the whole suburb seemed absolutely silent and deserted. Nebo said he would ride me round the gardens and then bring me back to Mrs. Owen's so that I could start work. I didn't ask him what the motoring get-up meant. I knew he wouldn't tell me the truth about it anyway.

The noisy cylinders burst into action at once. We circled the gardens quietly, at a slow pace, and then Nebo slipped his goggles over his eyes and we shot out on to the main road. We roared along it with tremendous acceleration out in the direction of the country, leaving the town behind us. At first, although I protested, I didn't really mind, the sensation of travelling at a high speed through the morning air I found exhilarating. There was no sign of life anywhere, not in houses or shops, we saw nobody at all except an occasional night-shift workman who stared at us.

Soon we had left the streets behind us and were charging along between fields and hedges. The morning was brilliant by now, very bright and sunny, but although I had the protection of Nebo's body I began to feel cold. Nebo took all the corners like a maniac, he never seemed to slacken his speed at all, he relied for our safety on the emptiness of the roads. In spite of my shouts and threats he showed no sign of returning. We left the main road and went deeper and deeper into a part of the country I had never been in before, an endless area of narrow twisted lanes and high hedges. I became more and more angry and alarmed, and as well I suffered very much now from the cold and the terrible jolting of the bike on the rough roads. "Hold on, Nebo," I shouted with my teeth rattling in my head. "Let's go back, shall we ? I want to do some reading before breakfast, you know."

"It's all right," he yelled sideways at me. "So do I. We'll turn round now in a minute. By the crossroads up there."

I looked forward over his shoulder, my body pressed close against his mackintosh for warmth, my eyes pouring water all the same. I began to feel rain on my face. In the mirror I could see the road pouring away behind us like a by-product. We shot over the crossroads without even slowing down.

Suddenly an old jibe of Nebo's flashed through my mind. "You're such a terrible sucker, Gari," he had jeered at me. "You must have been hard to wean." That was it. When I realized my own gullibility suddenly like that I became almost frantic with resentment. Nebo wasn't merely giving me a motor-bike ride, how could I ever have believed that even for a moment ; I was part, of course, of some considered plan of his, I was being used as everyone who came in contact with him was used. But how ? What was his scheme ? I could not even guess.

"Nebo," I shouted at him, really angry, "slow down, will you. If you don't, I'll lean over and get us both into the hedge."

Just as I said this the engine began to sputter exactly as it had done the day before, making a noise like a blade on a grindstone, and within a few yards the uproar and the jolting were over. We had come to rest at the roadside. What a relief. We dismounted and Nebo stood the bike on its rest. He took off his gauntlets and pushed up his goggles and stooped to examine the cylinders. The rain was falling although not heavily.

"Now what's the matter?" he said, his face going into extraordinary grimaces. I looked down angrily at him as he knelt there fiddling with plugs and cables, but although we were in this pickle, stranded in a country lane miles from my lodgings, I couldn't help being relieved and thankful to have my feet on firm ground again. In spite of feeling bitterly cold too, my teeth chattering and my eyes and nose watering freely in the cold air. In my relief at getting off the back of that awful bike I had forgotten for the moment my suspicions of Nebo. The sun had gone in and the rain was soon falling steadily. I knew nothing about motor-bikes so I began trotting up and down the deserted road trying to restore my heat. But the rain drove me for shelter under a tree near him after only two or three turns.

At last he said to me, "I'm awfully sorry about this, Gari. Were you enjoying it too? Honestly, I've no idea what's the matter. But I know what we can do if you'll help me. You remember that long hill we came up just now? Let's shove her back there and let her run down and then perhaps she'll start. Shall we try?"

"Why the devil did you bring me up here, Nebo?" I said to him. "I told you plenty not to. If I come out from under this tree I'll get soaked. Look at the rain."

But in the end I went. There was nothing else to do. Together we pushed the heavy machine back a few hundred yards along the flat until we came to the top of the long slope. Here Nebo tried again to kick the thing into action but it was still quite lifeless. The rain was falling in a heavy downpour by now, it was through my pyjamas of course and I was soaked to the skin.

He got astride and gave me my instructions. I was to run

81

behind him pushing, and the moment I heard the engine starting I was to give up at once and jump back on to my place behind him on the pillion. Never mind about the rain, he knew a short cut that would get us back to Mrs. Owen's in no time, in a matter of minutes. Everything would be fine.

I did exactly as I was told. I ran and pushed, the machine rolled pretty easily down the hill and within nine or ten yards the engine started with a tremendous roar. I was excited at this but I remembered what Nebo had said and ran along at the side of the bike and tried to climb on to the pillion. I received a violent blow on the chest from Nebo's side-swung arm. I stumbled and nearly went down on to the road. In a second or two I had recovered but the big bike had very rapid acceleration and before I could do anything it was roaring down the slope and in a minute or two it had disappeared round the bend.

*   *   *

It was breakfast time, nearly eight o'clock, when I reached Mrs. Owen's house.

After Nebo and the bike had disappeared it continued to rain heavily, a sort of silent thunderstorm with straight, icy thunder-rain. Down the road I could see a wooden platform with some milk churns on it, so I went along and crept in under it for shelter. I had given up trying to stop myself shivering. In about half an hour's time a milk lorry drove up and took the churns aboard. And the driver gave me a lift in it to right outside Mrs. Owen's door.

I felt very ill. Even in the warm cabin of the lorry I seemed to be hot and feverish and yet clammy and shivering at the same time. When Mrs. Owen answered the door to me she just stood staring, she couldn't believe her eyes. "Well, where have you come from ?" she said. "I thought you were upstairs in bed." It didn't seem to occur to her to do something, she just stood in the doorway and gazed. And there was I trembling violently from head to foot, and soaking wet, and dressed only in my pyjamas. "Mr. Davies has been here," she went on. "He told me not to disturb you. What happened ?"

By then I couldn't answer. I staggered forward and I would have collapsed on the floor of the hall but for her quickness. She half carried me into her kitchen where there was a good fire and got me to lie on the sofa. She loaded me with coats and bedclothes until I began to steam while she carried some hot-water bottles up to my bed. In a few minutes I dragged myself into the bedroom.

Mr. Herbert, I found the place in confusion. Although I was hungry for warmth and rest I began to examine the open drawers and cupboards and my clothes lying about the room in disorder. All my loose change was missing, the two pounds my mother had sent me to last the rest of the term, every shilling that was left of my scholarship grant, my watch, my cufflinks, my fountain pen, some of my books, all were gone. But Nebo hadn't taken all this trouble for the few pounds he could steal off me personally. He knew I had a good bit of money not my own in the room, it was the fifty odd pounds I was holding as treasurer of our honours class text-book fund. That too was gone. I sat down shivering on the edge of the bed and I'm afraid I wept.

Mrs. Owen was good to me then, I must agree. She gave me some tablets and when I had dried myself in the bathroom she got me to bed and piled clothes on me and drew the curtains against the daylight. After a time I went to sleep.

It was lunchtime when I awoke. Fortunately my exam didn't take place until the afternoon. I was feeling very ill, quite weak and feverish, but I got up, dressed and went downstairs.

There Mrs. Owen told me what had happened. She was sheepish doing it. Early that morning, she told me, when she was still in bed, she heard a knock at the front door. She found Nebo on the doorstep dressed in his motoring kit, something she had never seen him wearing before. He told her some yarn about his having been selected by the medical college to make a dash to Scotland with a rare drug. To save the life of a dying child. An only child. He was going on his motor-bike. Non-stop. Speed was everything. Could she lend him a fiver ? He would like to get one or two things from his room. He would not disturb Mr. Jeffreys. He went upstairs and returned with a full case that he strapped on the back of his bike.

Mrs. Owen confessed she had lent Nebo "over five pounds," but her pride, no doubt, wouldn't allow her to be more exact. She was shocked and humiliated at what had happened, at Nebo's lying, and his calculation and his cold-hearted duplicity. To think he could cheat and rob a man he had shared a room with, and whom he had known since childhood. My own emotions now were different. I found hard to bear the plain fact that, knowing Nebo intimately, I had accepted so readily the part he had laid out for me in this scheme of deceit and lying and theft. And I knew that the full result of my incredible foolishness was not yet to be seen. I still had my exams to sit and I felt less ready for them physically than I had ever done before.

One more thing happened that morning. When Mrs. Owen was bringing in my lunch she took a plate out of the cupboard with a couple of slices of bread on it I had forgotten about. Pinned on to the bread was a letter in Nebo's handwriting addressed to me. "Dear Gari," it said, "Ma Hartland was dead right. It caught up with me. By the time you read this I will be a married man. You have already met my wife. A charming girl, but frail. Almost, one might say, bracken was her downfall. Wish me luck. Excuse my writing—there's a tear in my eye."

It was signed "Nebo" and there were two postscripts. One said, "Best of luck in your exams. I hope your Mam soon has a first-class honours son." The second, "Talking about exams. It's dawned on me who the ' Woman of Kilmer Kyness ' is. A Jachbean play by one Thomas Heywood. ' A Woman Kilde with Kindness.' I must have got the name wrong. What a thought to guide a married man."

I have never seen Nebo since, Mr. Herbert. I struggled to attend all my exams although I was ill the whole time. At last, when I was back here in Ystrad, in hospital, recovering from pneumonia, I heard I had come out with a third. I knew this degree would be useless to me. I gave up all thought of an academic career and decided to return to this valley perman-ently. Through the influence of my father and his friends I was taken on at the colliery as a sort of apprentice mining engineer. I find the work interesting and I am less unhappy here now and less disappointed than I once was.

*   *   *

I don't know what has happened to Nebo, Mr. Herbert. His mother is dead now and nothing has been heard of him in the valley for many years. Whether he married that young woman or not, or whether he ever even intended to, I don't know. But I wouldn't be at all surprised to meet him back here in Ystrad some day. Nebo is quite shameless.

I remember once, though, when I was in London on a holiday, meeting Shenk Lewis, one of the men who had been at the university with Nebo and me. He had been very friendly with Nebo at one time, in fact, when his digs were next door to Tonza Griffiths's. Shenk was married and with a young family by the time I bumped into him, he was teaching German in South London, somewhere near Croydon, I think it was, and it was pleasant chatting to him about college friends that we hadn't seen for a few years. We had coffee together and during our talk I mentioned Nebo of course, and made one or two remarks about him. The name seemed to throw Shenk into a sort of frenzy, a misunderstanding of what I had said really. "Where did you see him, Gari ?" he said across the table in a kind of anguish. "*Where* did you see him ? Oh God, I hope I don't have to fall into his clutches again. I'll move. I'll leave London. Was it today you saw him ?"

I was astonished at the outburst. "I haven't seen Nebo, Shenk," I said. "Not since I left college. How did you think I had seen him ?"

I could see Shenk was making an effort of will to control himself. "I thought you said you had seen him," he said. "Didn't you say a minute ago you had been talking to him ?"

I reassured him and gradually he became calmer. But the charm of our meeting was gone. Shenk left me in a short time greatly disturbed, I could see, filled with forebodings and agonizing memories.

I sometimes wonder, Mr. Herbert, what I should do if I *were* to meet Nebo again. Should I try to revenge myself on him in any way, I wonder ? Or should I start laughing again at some fresh piece of lunacy he had become involved in. I hope I should have enough of my father's grace to do neither.

THE TOWER OF LOSS

It was a big surprise to Gronow and me when we recognised Loss Llewellyn rowing the boat.

The summer evening had turned out very placid and beautiful and as we came over the stepping-stones set in the mud down to the edge of the ferry, I was struck by the silence of the place; the absolute desolation all round us. The river was getting very wide there, it was like a broad lake, because its mouth and the open sea were only round the next curve of the hills, and a full tide was in it, the water moved slowly down past us in one solid mass, the surface flat and shiny, smooth as a mirror. The hills all round and the blue sky above were reflected in that glass, the slopes vivid green or eaten red with what looked like the rust of enormous sheets of tin or under big untidy fir plantations growing over the baldness, black and ragged like vast patches of buffalo wool right down to the water. There was no sound at all anywhere, only a gull sliding past us up the river every now and then, letting loose an occasional croak like a hinge-creak.

I stood by Gronow on the last of the stone slabs sunk to the level of the mud, right at the edge of the water, and bawled across the river for the ferry boat, which we had been told was kept on the far bank. My shouts carried pretty well in that stillness and before long we saw a man opening the door of a sort of stumpy lighthouse or low tower on the opposite bank and waving across to us. This tower was painted in broad prominent bands of black and white, you were bound to notice it because it was the only bit of masonry to be seen anywhere in the whole landscape. We watched the man hurrying along a little jetty in front of the tower, getting into his boat and starting to row across the river towards us.

Gronow and I were on a walking tour through this wild country of West Wales. Gronow was my friend, a broad plump man in a sort of tussore suit, a heavy figure with a belly and thick tight thighs. He had a large black head so solid his neck

87

had disappeared under it, it looked as though it had been squashed down into his trunk under the heavy weight resting on it. That belly started behind his shirt collar, it sloped gradually out towards you, flat as a drawing board, and swelled up the tussore into a sort of rubbery pregnancy. His fat face was swarthy and shapeless, always under a thick film of oil, and the fight he had had when young over a slighting review hadn't improved it. His nose was broken. Between his bouts of laughing his big mouth brought the swelling bulk of his lips together over a massive balcony of white teeth. As well as his yellow suit he was wearing heavy black boots and a fitter's blue shirt with pearly buttons ; also he carried his panama in his hand, showing his black hair sticking up stumpy on his head like something in the garden cut back for the winter. I watched him gazing out across the river at the black and white tower on the far bank, his little eyes glittering behind the horn-rimmed glasses.

I read somewhere or other that the muses love the warty boys. Gronow was at the time a rent collector in London and also a high-class Welsh poet. I had hardly read a line he'd written and we were friends because we came from the same mining valley, we had been at the grammar school together. But I had always studied the notices of his books with interest and they seemed to make him out to be some sort of literary freak, a bit of a monster almost, it seemed to me, a mixture, one of the critics said, of poetic toryism, dandyism and exoticism. Something like that. I wasn't a poet and I couldn't understand it properly. But as I watched him standing there beside me on that bottom slab by the water I thought what they said meant the whole scene before us, every image and sparkle of it, most likely, was being tucked away, blink by blink, through those black-rimmed glasses and into the beady little eyes glittering away non-stop behind them.

Because in spite of the desolation all round us this was a pretty impressive sort of scene to be mixed up in. Half the blue sky in front of us above the river was filled up with one massive cloud, a great white mass like a complete mountain range of ballooned-out ivory ; every glade and cliff and summit of it was delicately silvered, it had its own clouds hiding its own peaks, and the whole radiant mass moved majestically up the valley above the water like some range of fancy mountains towed inland from the sea. And at the same time, at the edge of the wood we had just come through, a thrush was singing, sending his summer passion down my spine like slow ice. I glanced at Gronow again to see how he was taking it. His face was almost expressionless under the shine of grease but his nostrils were fluttering, I could see his belly rising and falling in a rapid kicking rhythm he was trying hard to control. He pointed out across the ferry, his laugh very quiet, making a soft hooting noise with a bit of a hiss in it.

The boat we had seen the man on the opposite bank row out from the jetty had reached mid-stream by now, but it wasn't coming across in our direction any more. It looked like some demented beetle performing a series of idiotic tacking motions in the middle of the river. At the same time it was drifting further downstream at a good speed, it looked as though before long it would disappear round the bend and float out helpless into the open sea. As we watched, the boatman seemed to realise this danger himself because he began to pull on the oars like mad, for twenty yards he came up the middle of the river rowing like a maniac. But when he was once more right opposite our stepping stones, travelling at a good speed, suddenly the boat stopped absolutely dead ; it came to a halt with such a jerk the stern reared up out of the water with the shock of it. And at the same moment we had a lightning glimpse of the boatman pitching over backwards on to the floorboards with his seaboots in the air. Both his oars rose up helplessly as though they were washing their hands of the whole business and floated slowly away on the water looking exhausted and despondent.

Then every single hair on my head was driven like pins and needles into my scalp with fright. The boatman scrambled to his feet and, without hesitating for a second, sprang overboard fully clothed with a big splash right in the middle of the river. I shouted out with excitement, but the water didn't rise above his calves. He paddled down on the hidden sandbank after the oars and when he'd put them back on board he leaned forward and began pushing the boat towards us from the stern, he didn't get back in, he came calmly through the water leaning against the back end rather like someone wheeling a railway tea-wagon in front of him up the station platform.

Gronow had retired to a log at the edge of the wood. He sat there speechless beside our knapsacks, his heavy cropped head propped between his hands, and his shoulders shaking as though he was shedding a heavy drench of laughing. He was helpless.

The boatman came on, pushing, until he was within about twenty yards of the stepping stones. Then, seeming to want to round off his lunacy—or perhaps the water got much deeper again there—he jumped back aboard and rowed in to the shore. And then I recognized him, I could see that the erratic ferryman, the lunatic in the navy jersey and the sea-boots, was Loss Llewellyn with his beard shaved off.

*   *   *

Before the war I used to meet Loss very often in the flat of a man I lodged with when I was working in London selling typewriters.

This man's name was Hoverington. He was supposed to be a bit of a yogi or something, and he wrote a very philosophic type of poetry, it had no rhymes and was very spaced out on the pages. He and his wife Tessa, a nice red-headed slut she was, lived in an enormous attic flat, a great green barn of a place with wooden walls about three feet high and all the windows in the roof. They were always in heavy debt and having dead-born babies. In some ways lodging with them was pretty inconvenient. The door of my bedroom, for instance, would never close properly, the room was so small that the foot of the bed came out permanently on to the landing. Then every single thing that Tessa cooked tasted queer, her meals made you think of sweet timber in slices or else a cut off a cold poultice. They hadn't got one complete set of crockery in the place or even a knife that didn't turn sideways in the handle when you pressed on it. Often you had to use your shaving-stick to bath with because there was no soap, and in the jakes you'd only find a few sheets of cardboard, or perhaps a blue sugar-bag or a lump of wadding from inside the baby's teddybear. Once, stubbed out round the handbasin in the bathroom, I counted thirty-five cigarette ends—and two slices of beetroot.

But Hoverington was a wonderful character, he was always serene and quite willing for everything. When I talked to Gronow about him he only jeered. "Hoverington's a spineless slug," he said. "Hoverington!"

"You can't see anything good in poise and magnanimity, can you, you rude ape," I answered, a bit rattled.

"Anybody can be like Hoverington who's had the cheesy life he's had," Goronw grinned. "He wasn't brought up in the Valleys. He knows nothing. He lives on top of the hedge and blows about with every breeze. Has he ever put one foot past the other to help anybody at all? Shitten Hoverington!"

I remember the first night I brought Gronow up to my lodgings, it was to a party by invitation of Hoverington who always wanted to meet poets and painters and that. Gronow, poor dab, was speechless after fetching his big bulk up the half dozen flights of stairs leading to the Hoverington's flat. When we got inside, the whole place was in darkness, apart from a candle burning on a saucer, that is, and the glow of the gas fire. As usual there was a powerful smell of babies. By the light of the fire I could make out Tessa beside it smoking a cigarette, she was stripped to the waist and giving suck to a baby that had managed somehow, so far anyway, to survive her good nature. Hoverington himself was only a cigarette-glow in the gloom and when he heard us coming in he called us towards him, welcoming us in the sort of posh soothing voice he had. I felt pretty certain he would be flat out on the settee wearing his ragged green tweeds and his black polo-neck pullover and the gilded sandals some Indian disciple of his had given him. And I guessed too that he and Tessa had run out of shillings for the electric light again. I put a couple of bob in the metre behind the landing door and the powerful glare pounced into the room from the two unshaded bulbs hung from the rafters.

I could see Gronow blinking behind his glasses. But he took it all in, the big resounding attic as bare as a barn and much shabbier, the drab three feet high wall-boards painted committee-room green, the cracky sky-lights, the silk stockings drying on the candle-brackets of the piano, the parrot-cage hanging from the tie-beam with a half-dead rabbit in it. He took Tessa in too. "She's a nice sort of girl, Tessa," he used to say about her after. "It's a pity she can't understand the baby's bottom is more important than its face. But she's very nice is Tessa, poor little sod."

"I'm glad you've been able to come," Hoverington said, waving his cigarette to us from the settee. "Dewi has told me a lot about you. My wife, Tessa. Gronow Lloyd the Welsh poet. Please do sit down, won't you?"

I saw Gronow bowing and, still pretty blown, looking round, anxious to sit down anywhere after that climb. But the orange-box furniture and the three chairs were all heavily under books, papers, magazines, used crockery and Tessa's underclothes. So to give him a lead I did what Hoverington always expected his guests to do when he was lying comfortable on his settee. I sat down on the floor. But I was careful to go down on one of the home-made rope mats they had about the place. I had been in Hoverington's flat long enough to know that half his friends suffered from crippling rheumatic pains in the hams through sitting in the fresh air that came whistling up through the cracks between his bare floorboards.

"Don't bother about me," Gronow panted, "I'll lean."

In his tight black coat and striped trousers and his nail-brush hair he looked a bit out of it, he reminded me somehow in his working clothes of a low-grade football tout, or still more of a shady faith-healer. As he rolled off to take up his position leaning in the corner I saw him breaking into a little trot, something had happened to the flooring in that part of the attic and the boards dipped downhill into the wall at a big angle.

"We've got another countryman of yours coming along in a few minutes," Hoverington said to Gronow. "A painter. Carlos Llewellyn. Do you know him?"

I had met Loss many times of course but Gronow shook his head and lumbered back up the slope again to open the door to let Tessa out. What the devil was he grinning at, I wondered. I hoped it was only at his little trot when he ran downhill into the wall, or rather the ceiling.

In appearance this Hoverington was pretty unremarkable. His body was long, thin and limp, he lay now stretched out flat on the settee in his terrible old patched up suit and his black ganzy. When you saw his head like this, from a point near the floor, it looked thin and supple, soft, a bit like a snake's, hardly more than a thickened out extension of his long thin neck. His hair was thin and puffy, very unsubstantial, unattached to his scalp somehow, like a cloud floating about around the summit of a high mountain. His profile always looked to me slightly adenoidal. Hoverington had that half-strangled look you see on those side-faces the phoneticians use on their charts, when they want to show you the proper way to manage the larynx and the vocal cords. And, of course, he had completely swallowed his chin. Only Hoverington's eye, I always felt, set in a skin the colour of old dough, saved him from looking absolutely wet. But even this eye never seemed quite normal, not an object that sensation was passing into ; more like it was something itself steadily pouring out a powerful beam of dotty good-nature.

Soon the other guests began to arrive. A lot of the Hoveringtons' friends seemed to be cranks of some sort, or maniacs almost, and I was connected with their world really only through my lodgings and the typewriters and stuff I sometimes managed to sell them. One of the visitors that night again was Max, a sculptor who never seemed to sculpt anything, a chap who always came with a couple of bottles of gin in his pockets and sometimes bellowed about the attic like a stung bull. Another was an unpublished novelist, baring his teeth all the time in a way that made you think of an intelligent horse drinking. Another was an Indian poet who was always getting caught scratching dirt on the walls of the public dubliws. The dirt was in Greek but that didn't stop the poor chap getting convicted.

All these, and the others, Hoverington called over the boards in turn to meet Gronow and I watched the ones who were seeing him for the first time whispering to one another after the meeting and looking puzzled.

Because Gronow that night, as I say, was wearing his working clothes, his tight black coat and vest and striped trousers. He had brought his rent-collecting ledgers with him, stuffed into the special pockets inside his jacket, and these gave his trunk several large flat planes with upright edges, there were smooth surfaces round his body that made him look a bit like the stump of a six-sided pencil. With his oily skin and his big mouth and his broken nose he didn't make you think much of the dazzling sort of figure the reviewers made him out to be. He was a real puzzle. And his laugh as well didn't help, it had something very unsettling and jeering in it.

People kept on arriving until between twenty and thirty squatted down on the floor or stood about smoking and drinking and jawing at the tops of their voices. Tessa was soon back in the room wearing a green quilted dressing gown, she looked very picturesque as usual under her auburn halo of hair ; and Hoverington still lay stretched out comfortably on the settee, listening. He didn't say much, he just idled there under the light of the naked bulb, smoking a cigarette with a big bend in it, swivelling his huge pale eyes slowly around the room like the benevolent beams of a lighthouse.

And at last Loss Llewellyn came into the tobacco smoke, hand in hand with the girl he was living with, the one everybody called Jersey. He was in his colours, wearing a salmon-pink shirt, a thick purple tie, a sky blue jacket and sandals. He had small gold ear-rings in his ears. His beard was black and silky and so was his hair, but in spite of this, and in spite of his tall figure too, Loss never managed to look dashing at all, or piratical, or anything like that. For one thing his eyes had a bleached look and the outlines of his skin and jaw, which you could see clearly through his thin beard, looked pretty meagre, and his pink nose wasn't much help to him or his top teeth hanging out as though he was giving them an airing all the time he wasn't talking. But the people who came to Hoverington's flat always treated Loss with a lot of respect. For one thing he had money, and for another he was always telling everybody he had dedicated his whole life absolutely and irrevocably to painting.

I think they called Loss's girl Jersey because she was supposed to be like that actress who was the fancy of one of the kings. To me, what with the band she always wore round her forehead and her long, loose, sack-like dresses hung everywhere with long fringes, she looked more like a stage Red Indian. But she wasn't dark, she had a mass of light golden hair which billowed below her head-band all round her pink high-class face. She was easily the most beautiful girl that came to the Hoveringtons, very tall and slender and elegant, more beautiful than Tessa even, or anyway more superior looking. She never said a word to anybody. All she wanted was for everybody to take notice of her all the time. One night very late when half a dozen of us, Hoverington's friends, were walking along the empty street arguing like mad about something or other we forgot she was with us, for four or five minutes nobody said a word to her. She walked on ahead of us and fell in a heap on the pavement. We all ran up to her but we saw soon enough there was nothing much the matter with her. After we petted her a bit she was all right—but she made Loss call a taxi and take her home in it all the same.

Hoverington waved Loss and Jersey forward and introduced Gronow to them. Loss squeezed down on the floor beside me under the roof of Gronow's belly and Jersey sat beside him. At first all Loss did was frown in the middle of all the talking, he was quiet and reserved, very moody, he went on turning one of his ear-rings round and round in the lobe of his ear and fiddling with his beard. But after a few swigs from the sculptor's bottle he found his tongue and he began to explain some theory or other he had about poetry, for Gronow's benefit I thought, he brought Shakespeare into it when he was a homosexual, and Byron sleeping with his sister, and John Ruskin because he was impotent and mad. And that poet Swinburne was mixed up in it too after a bit, somehow, because he was forty before he knew where his bladder was ; and some writer I'd never heard of who lost his nose through an attack of the pox. That was one of the best things about Hoverington's lodgings, I always used to think, you would never hear any talk there except about culture. Anyway, when this was going on, Gronow, behind us, got cornered by a couple of young women, a pair of poetic twins who often came to the Hoveringtons', real tuft-hunters they were, "intense, tow-haired and titless" Gronow said after, they were trying to get him to discuss some theory or other they had, but he wasn't interested, I could hear him saying, "Yes, yes, yes," indifferent, most likely bored.

After a bit the bedlam in the room began to die down, the hush seemed to be spreading from somewhere round about the settee where Hoverington was lying ; he was holding a very thick sort of magazine in his hand and reading out of it in that thrilling organy voice that was really the poshest thing about him. He had put his glasses on and because of that he could only read with one eye. He had accidentally snapped off the right-hand side-piece of his specs a couple of months before and to use them now he had to tie a length of red darning wool round the nose-piece, pull it taut across his eyeball and use his right ear as a cleat to twist it round and round.

The first words I actually heard Hoverington read out began with, "For sex is the over-riding problem of our generation, as faith was that of our grandfathers'."

Loss stopped talking at once at this. Hoverington gave out the sentences very slow and solemn, his voice rose and fell in a real parsonish singsong, you could swear he was reading some extra heavy bit out of one of those eastern books of religious meditation he was so fond of, or even one of his own poems. Everybody in the attic sat absolutely absorbed and silent in no time, after a few more of Hoverington's sentences the jabbering stopped altogether, the cups and bottles were lowered to the boards and on the faces of all the listeners around me I could see the serious expressions, very grave and solemn, and sort of devotional.

I glanced round at Gronow. He had shaken off the twins and had been talking to the rabbit in the bird-cage with his back to us. I could see his shoulders were shaking. Gronow had two laughs. One was a sort of outburst of coarse guffaws, very startling and upsetting, he was speechless when this struck him, and helpless, all he could do was sit down until the fat on him stopped quaking a bit and the convulsions quietened down to normal. His other laugh was usually a sort of overture to this, it was almost silent, only a long hoarse sound came out of his throat, it sounded a bit like the brassy hiss of a bugle when somebody blows into it without enough

96

wind to make the proper note. I was pretty well attuned to Gronow in those days and it was this hoarse hissing sound that I began to hear now coming out of him.

In the meantime Hoverington's sentences went on. The atmosphere in the attic seemed very religious and devotional, you could think you were in a real prayer-meeting. Heads were nodding reverentially all round, one or two of the listeners even started hear-hearing—only it was so much like a meeting house you felt they ought to be saying amen. And then the writer reached the high spot of his article, he began maintaining, in what I thought was a pretty eloquent and convincing way, that the dimensions of the male organ *can* under suitable treatment, with diet and exercise, be greatly increased.

Fair play, that brought the religious atmosphere to its most intense, I could feel it in the silence like a revival. But Gronow failed to hold in any longer, his awful guffawing laugh and the echoes it made everywhere resounded through the hushed attic, he began moving across the room looking clumsy and loutish, and signalling me to the door.

Hoverington stopped reading and waited. He was still serene and unmoved on the settee, all he did was pass his hand through the thin cloud-cap of his locks in slight embarrassment and jerk his golden sandal up and down a bit. But his guests looked bewildered, some of them, others red and angry ; the sculptor glared towards the door and the poetic twins hunched together like moping poultry, they raised up identical eyebrows, indignant and severe.

Gronow waited for me with his hand on the door-knob. He couldn't say a word. He stood with his big white teeth bulging out of his face and his skin drenched with grease. He was managing by now not to make any sound although his belly kicked up and down all the time under the ledgers. When I got to him he flashed his glasses round at everybody, waved his hand and went down the stairs.

Out in the street he clung to my arm. All the time the laughs were rising in his throat. When he was a bit calmer he outlined a poem he was going to write for chanting, with a chorus denouncing religion, justice, peace, philosophy and that, and proclaiming the primacy of the external genitalia. I saw him on to his bus and then went back to my lodgings.

All the guests had gone. Hoverington was still calm and unmoved on his sofa, I searched him but I couldn't see the smallest dot of resentment in his eye. All he did was ask me if I could spare him a few cigarettes until the morning.

*   *   *

Loss Llewellyn always like to be on the jeering side, I knew that, and I never saw him at any of Hoverington's parties after that night. But Gronow and I used to bump into him often in other people's places and he began to surprise us by taking an interest in our background, the sort of way we had been brought up and that, so different from his own childhood in a mansion in some posh Sussex village. Then one day when we hadn't seen him for two or three months, we got a long letter from him telling us about a new religion he'd found and asking us down to his place to hear more about it. He told us he'd given up painting altogether, he had sold his studio and returned to his native country, to Wales, to live there among the workers of one of the Dinas dockland slums. The letter was full of Loss's usual big talk and up-to-date jargon, so modern you could hardly understand it. What was the use, he asked us, of applying paint to canvas in a world free-wheeling to disaster? Only political action was logical and satisfying ; the inflated ego of the artist was an anachronism ; Loss was determined, a dedicated soul, to march forward in the van of the class which had history on its side. Did we realize the conditions in which millions still lived ? Mrs. Moncrieff on the floor of the tenement below him was so poor she had swallowed a bottle of disinfectant when she knew her tenth was on the road ; and the Johnsons next door had tried to bury their baby in some garden when it died of malnutrition, because they couldn't raise the price of a funeral . . .

Gronow and I knew all about this, we had known it all our lives. To us Loss sounded as though he'd gone a bit odd, but we decided to pay him a visit the next time we were in Wales, it would be interesting hearing this stuff straight from the lips of somebody so unlikely as Loss Llewellyn.

98

It was early evening when our bus got into the Dinas dockland area where Loss lived then, the sky was transparent yellow, like a long glass dish of lemonade. From the rise in the road over the railway bridge we could see the whole steaming mass of dockland brickwork below us, grey and shapeless, like something the city had had back on the foreshore.

The area Loss told us he lived in was called Tiger Bay, it was mostly made up of shabby houses and cafes and ships' chandlers and shops selling oilskins and groceries and engine valves and boiler piping. Groups of seamen, many of them coloured, lounged idle at every corner and coloured children ran about screaming or chalking their games on the pavements. Every building seemed old and shabby and run-down. In the bare front windows of the cafes we could see an aspidistra perhaps, and a plate of fly-blown rock-cakes, and inside a few drabs with pimples and untidy hair sitting round the fire.

We found Loss's street and went in to his address through a dark passage alongside a barber's shop. "If I know anything about this sort of place," Gronow said, "we'd better light a couple of pipes before we go any further." We went up the pitch-black wooden stairs, several flights of them, to a small landing surrounded by doors and with a skylight overhead. Here the smell of stale fish was strong in spite of our pipes, but Gronow only grinned as he looked round, his face gleaming as though it had been basted.

On one of the doors on the landing we found Loss's number, seventeen, tacked on in tin figures, but the door was fastened with a padlock and a galvanised chain that went in through a hole burnt in the panel and out through another between the doorpost and the wall. There was no answer when we knocked. We tried next door where we could hear a melodeon playing "Jack o' Diamonds" but we had no luck there either ; nor at the next door where a kid was grizzling, nor the next where a man and woman were having a knock-about quarrel. That left us only one more door on that landing to knock at. When Gronow failed to get an answer he quietly turned the knob and looked in.

It was dim and bare inside and the room was lit only by a bats-wing burner with a wire ball around it. It stank of bloaters. Here and there big pieces of plaster had dropped off the wet walls showing the lath ribs. A man sat at a table with his back to us reading a newspaper.

"Excuse me, please," Gronow said, leaning in, his hand still on the door-knob, "I wonder if you could help us."

The man turned round in time, got up from his chair and very slowly padded over the floor towards us, bringing his paper with him.

He was a very peculiar sort of chap, he must have been the greyest man in dockland. He was short but he seemed to loom up towards us like some ancient mud-monster with this powerful fishy smell about him and dried-hard sludge making up his flesh and everything he wore on it. He came on at a sort of slow boxer's crouch, his knees bent, his long arms dangling, his feet in their slippers dragging on the floor as though they didn't want to come apart from their native slime. He was wearing grey corduroy trousers and a dark grey flannel shirt, both of them dirty and shapeless, and a colourless muffler went round his neck instead of a collar and tie. His waistcoat shone like oilskin and hung open, the two sides anchored together by a big brass watch-chain. He was a good bit undersized as to height but very heavy, and very bulky in the trunk. All his baggy old skin was grey, and wrinkled as dried-out mud-banks, his big stupid face was unshaven and covered with a mass of muddy puckers. A grey fringe went round his bald head above his thick quilted-looking ears and he had a grey walrus moustache.

I saw Gronow twinkling down at this sort of mud-made prodigy, his nostrils fluttered and his mouth seemed ready to fly open any minute and let his teeth come through.

"Oh, ah!" the man said, coming to rest from his clumsy shamble and shooting us off with his paper. "Ah'm not signing, mister, Ah'm not signing. Ah'll take my oath on that."

His voice was very hoarse and sudden, but resonant, he sounded a bit like those ball-balancing sea-lions giving out in their excitement a series of asthmatic barks.

Gronow took no notice of the shooing off. "We are trying to find a friend of ours called Llewellyn," he said. "I wonder if you could help us."

The man scowled up at us, from Gronow to me and back again, and his lower jaw began a slow sideways chewing action. He looked bewildered.

"Liwellian," he said, "Liwellian, did you say ? Oh, ah ! No, Ah don't know no Liwellian round here."

"No ?" said Gronow. "The address we were given was in this building. Number seventeen. Tall and dark. With gold ear-rings."

"With gold ear-rings, mister ?" the man repeated. "With gold ear-rings ? No, there's no Mrs. Liwellian in this house, no Mrs. Liwellian here, mister."

Every time he stopped talking his mouth began this slow cud-chewing motion, his bristly bottom jaw went meditatively from side to side under the big moustache like the mouth of a cow.

"No, no," Gronow said, grinning. "It's a man. With a black beard. Tall, dark. *Mr.* Llewellyn."

"*Mr.* Liwellian," he replied. "*Mr.* Liwellian. With gold ear-rings." He stopped and scowled again from Gronow to me and back again, very suspicious. And then the idea seemed to amuse him a bit, for a second or two there was a break in the dense mud-like cakings of the skin of his face. "No," he went on, sober again, "there's no Mr. Liwellian in this house, Ah'll take my oath on that now. Never was a Mr. Liwellian in this house, mister."

"Is this the man with history on his side ?" Gronow said to me in Welsh, grinning. "Shall we give him the bullet or try him again ? I feel sure there used to be a Mr. Llewellyn here," he said to the man. "Tall, dark, with ear-rings and a beard."

"Tell him about the workers," I suggested. "A great one for the workers," I said to the man. "A leader."

He folded up his newspaper. His grey shirt-sleeves were rolled up to the elbows and the outsides of both his arms were covered with a mass of dull blue and red tattoos, and so was his chest. After a bit of pondering a faint gleam shot out of the wrinkles.

"Oh, ah !" he barked hoarsely. "Mr. Liwellian did you say, mister ? Ah though you said Liwellian. Ah know **Mr.** Liwellian right well now."

101

Gronow looked at me and grinned.

"Well," he said, "can you tell us where Mr. Liwellian might be ? Honestly," he said to me, "I meant to say Llewellyn."

"No," he replied, nodding. "No, Ah don't know where he might be now, mister."

There was a pause for a bit again and the three of us stood without saying a word. The cud-chewing under the big hairy mainsail of the moustache began again and every now and then we were belched at with bloatery breath. Gronow sucked his pipe hard and began to explain, very patient he was, what it was all about and what we wanted to do.

"It would," the man said at last, "Mr. Liwellian's door would be locked now. Mr. Liwellian went into hospital these ten days gone, they say."

"Into hospital" we said together. "What's the matter with him ?"

"Mr. Liwellian's in hospital now," he said, "because he was hit over the head with a bottle."

"Hit over the head !" said Gronow. "With a bottle ? How did that happen ?"

"Was it a riot or something ?" I asked. "Police and the workers ? A clash ?"

Again that look of faint amusement broke through the wrinkles. "Oh, ah ! No !" he said, and the barks sounded a bit brighter. "He wasn't with the workers when he got hit, Ah'll take my oath on that now." He puckered his face up at us. "Mister," he said to Gronow, "it was a worker what hit him with the bottle."

"A worker hit him ?" said Gronow. "Why ? Was there a fight or something ?"

"A fight ! No ! There weren't no fight now."

"Well what then ?"

"Mr. Liwellian was met coming out of the Owens' room."

"Yes ?"

"And Owens was coming ashore earlier than expected."

"And Owens is a married man ?"

"Oh, ah ! Ah'll take my oath on that—Owens is a married man."

"And big ?" I asked.

"Oh, ah, mister," he answered. "And black. Big and black, that's Ali Owens."

I could feel Gronow's belly at my elbow beginning to fluctuate and the sort of soft hooting began to blow past my ear. He turned away without saying any more and went back out on to the landing. I thanked our man but he didn't seem willing to let us go now.

"Mister," he said to me, padding out on to the landing after us, "Ah thought you was from the shipping. That's what Ah thought you was, mister."

"You're a seaman, are you ?" I asked him, beginning to follow Gronow down the stairs.

"Ah'm a donkeyman. That's what I am, mister, a donkeyman."

My head was level with his slippers. I asked him what hospital Loss had been taken to. Gronow had gone down into the darkness but his pipe-smoke floated back up the staircase. "Oh, ah ! No ! Ah don't know which hospital he was took to," he barked at me. "Ah thought you was the company, mister."

I took another few steps down. I couldn't see the old man any more. "Ah thought you two was the company," he barked down after us. "And Ah'm not going to sea in the flat-racing season, Ah'll take my oath on that."

Gronow heard. His laugh went past me up the stairs, it sounded like the crazy uproar of a brick howling down a disused airshaft.

We heard later that Loss had retired to the country but we never set eyes on him again until after the war when we met him at the ferry that lovely evening during our walking tour in West Wales.

*   *   *

In spite of everything, the journey over the river in the evening sunlight was very pleasant.

I sat on the stern thwart of Loss's little rowing boat with our knapsacks beside me and Gronow got up in the bows. Loss didn't look much of a ferryman to me. The inside of the boat was swimming with water and it wasn't easy finding a decent bit of dry seat to sit down on. Loss was facing me and as he rowed I could see he was trying to look very intent all the time, as though he was absorbed in some heavy private business or other, very solemn and important. But he was nervous or clumsy or something. Every time the boat wobbled a bit or the oars jerked out of the rowlocks he had to shoot me a very self-conscious look from under the brim of his sou'wester to see if I had noticed.

Without his beard his face looked meagre, childish, I thought, and the cold pink hump of his nose seemed to be all over it. The holes in the lobes of his ears were empty and he had clipped back his eyebrows like moustaches. The expression he tried to keep on his face was humble, he looked meek and long suffering, he seemed to be trying to give us the idea his mind was busy milling very pure thoughts all the time and there was an expression of patience and understanding in his silver eyes when he turned them up to the sky.

The evening was lovely, very cool and dead silent on the water. Ahead of the boat the brown cliff on the far side of the river was receiving the full blaze of the setting sun, it seemed to glow like a wall of dusty bronze. The sky by now was almost everywhere blue and clear, very radiant, and only a few clouds were floating there, as transparent as steam. I could see a heron sunning himself on his little beach below the cliff, parading the sand as slow and dignified as a cigar-smoker. As Loss pulled at the oars the water bulged up before the bows of the boat and spread out when we cut through, frilly and tinkling on both sides of us. The breeze was delicate coming off the sea, it went over the skin as smooth as milk. In his tight tussore suit, looking like two cushions stuffed into one cover, Gronow sat facing the light, he was bareheaded and grinning, his glasses flashing and the shiny lubrication coming out all over his face.

We still had three or four miles to walk after getting out of the boat, Loss told us, before we reached the village we meant to spend the night at. When we asked him about the road he stood up to point, we were in midstream at the time and the boat began rocking like mad and the water from the oars added to what was already slopping about in the bottom. He showed us our road curving over the hills like a flat snake and dangling its tail down into a near-by plantation. He was very sorry he couldn't have us to stay with him, but there was only room in his tower for himself, worse luck. He was practically a hermit, he lived absolutely alone, he saw nobody now except the few local people he ferried over the river. He had cut himself off completely from his old life, from politics, from art, from painting, with another ex-artist he could say, "Je ne m'occupe plus de cela." Did we still know Hoverington, with his pathetic concern for art, and his theories, and his parties ? What was his latest craze, was it brewing herbs ? Or mat-making ? Or bottling that ghastly home-made carrot wine, or what ?

I told him I didn't live with the Hoveringtons any more, my territory had been changed, but I still saw them from time to time. Gronow sat grinning up there in the bows behind Loss, his glasses signalling like twin heliographs in the sun. He wanted to know how Loss came to be in this no-man's land. What about the workers ? Had their cause triumphed at last, or what ?

Loss bared his hanging teeth at me in a slow smile, full of calm and patience and understanding. As he spoke he made out he'd learnt some deeper wisdom among his own people, here amid the remote solitude and grandeur of his native hills. As long as his tower stood and gave him shelter he would continue to live in this place and serve the people. With a soppy sort of look he sketched out his conversion. During his illness, brought about as a result of living in slum conditions, he had had a vision of what life for him should be from then on. He knew for a certainty that he had been called and chosen, that his days were to be spent exclusively in service, and what he called expiation.

These words coming from Loss made me feel pretty uncom-fortable, especially as Gronow's grin, instead of getting less with respect and understanding, was taking in wider areas of his face-fat. He was very interested to hear that, he said, speaking into the back of Loss's neck. He had often wished the flow of his own thoughts could change its bed somehow, and that he could inhabit such exalted planes of experience himself. But having to work for a living, he always felt, tended to coarsen one, and to bring one all the time into contact with what was cheapest and crudest and most sordid in life. Didn't Loss agree with him ?

Loss had never done a day's work in his life but he did agree and he also said we must never forget there was always compensation in the dignity and nobility of labour.

For instance, Gronow went on, ignoring him, how was it possible to devote oneself to the real problems of existence when one was subject to the experiences encountered in rent-collecting ? Only the week before our tour started, he said, he had gone into a substantial sort of villa in suburban London and asked for the rent. A big hard-faced bossy-looking woman showed him in, she put him in a large front room, dim and very raffish, her huge soft bosom quaked when she was doing it as though she had loaded a couple of gallons of upright jelly into her dressing-gown. She told him to sit down, if he would excuse her she wouldn't be long getting the money. After a bit of delay and whispering in the passage the door opened and a beautiful girl walked into the room grinning, wearing a man's long dressing-gown. She came round and stood on the carpet in front of Gronow. Then she slipped her dressing-gown off and underneath she was naked, she didn't have a stitch of clothing on apart from a pair of fishnet stockings.

By this time Loss had stopped rowing and was turning his head sideways so that he could hear better. Gronow grinned over at me.

"Yes, yes," said Loss, "go on. What happened then ?"

Gronow laughed. "Nothing," he said. "I had fifty quid of rents in my pocket. But how disturbing for me."

Loss saw he had been hoaxed and began to row again. The slum-dwellers, he told us, he found brutish and unresponsive, indifferent to sacrifice and the generosity of disinterested action. But now, he felt, his life, however remote and obscure, was one of serene contemplation and service and fulfilment.

Bit by bit, as we got nearer the jetty below the black and white tower, Loss told us the story of the place we were in. An ancestor of his, a landowner in these parts a century ago, had promised the farmers he would build a bridge across the river for their use—he had put twenty thousand pounds aside for it—if they would return him to parliament as their member when the time came. He lost the contest by about twenty votes and to spite the electors what the old chap did was to build a huge folly at the river's edge just where the bridge ought to have been, he spent the twenty thousand pounds on a lot of useless roofless buildings and miles and miles of walls with nothing inside them. As time went on the folly gradually disappeared, the farmers all round began to use it as a quarry, they carted whole buildings away stone by stone to patch up their homes and extend their outhouses ; and now, after more than a hundred years, almost everything had disappeared, only the tower Loss lived in was still in one piece. Lying sick in hospital he had determined to dedicate his life to, as he said, the expiation of this act of ancestral vindictiveness ; since he couldn't afford to build the bridge himself he meant to devote the remainder of his days, an inglorious Welsh Christopher perhaps, to ferrying the people of the neighbourhood and their goods across the river. In this remote spot, once the home of his fathers, forgotten by the world, he was passing his days now alone in service and contemplation and renunciation.

I got my eyes away from Gronow's grinning face. We were rapidly approaching the shore and I could see the details of the stumpy tower. It had a low pointed slate roof and one or two tiny windows, and those alternate bands of what looked like white lime and tar around it which we had seen from the other bank. Surely I could make out a head at the middle window—or was it a flowerpot ? On the jetty where we were going to land two young women were standing in the sunlight waiting to cross. In a few minutes Loss got the boat somehow alongside the wooden landing stage.

The two girls were young and pretty, one dark and one auburn, they looked like farm girls coming back from the village where we hoped to stop for the night. One of them carried a big empty butter basket and the other was in trouble with a new pair of heavy hobnailed farm-boots, the backs threaded together with twine. They giggled a lot and the colour rose in their cheeks as Loss handed them into the boat in our places after we got out, he was tall and solemn doing it in his sou'-wester and blue jersey and we could see he was enjoying it, especially pocketing the fare. They went to the dry places we had left, the auburn sat in Gronow's seat in the front and the dark one went back to the stern, and we passed the square basket and the boots in after them. They seemed to be enjoying themselves too, they laughed and blushed and giggled all the time, but they didn't say much. When they spoke it was in Welsh. Loss apologised for having to leave us at once in this way, but he hoped we would forgive him. We would be certain to reach the village before nightfall now. Goodbye. He was glad to have seen us again. No, no. No charge of course. Goodbye. Goodbye.

We pushed him off and waved to the girls as he paddled out into the river and then we walked up the jetty towards the shore. The tower was at the far end of a little path that sloped up from the jetty to its tarred door. It must have been a head I had seen at the window because it wasn't there any longer. We passed close to the glistening door and I couldn't help noticing that the doorstep under it was well-worn and hollowed out, it looked a bit like a bottom lip in a kind of wry grin.

After leaving the path we went over some beds of bladder-wrack that Gronow didn't enjoy, he said it was like treading on a squash of bowels, but we were soon on the hard sand where I had seen the heron, and I found it pleasant walking there in the sunlight at the side of the river. Gronow sloped along beside me, to balance the mass of heavy flesh he carried in front of him he always moved along leaning slightly backwards, the angle of his body to the earth made him look rakish like the masts of a schooner.

From this little beach below the cliff we could see the woods opposite across the water and the line of the stepping-stones we had used coming down from them to the edge of the river. There was a ploughed field on the hill behind the woods, the furrows rigid as harp strings, and the blue mountains were like a batter in the distance all around. As we looked, a full blackbird flew past us quite close with his chin up, making a loud clinking noise, and he drew our attention back to the water.

Loss's boat was by now a fair distance out in the river, it was broadside on to us and at a standstill. The two girls looked as if they were trying to change places, they were both on their feet, the auburn-haired boot-carrier was struggling towards the stern and the dark one was groping her way towards the bows at a crouch. When they met in the middle where Loss was sitting they clung together giggling and the boat began to rock violently. Loss, as though he meant to steady them, got up on his feet. The next minute both the girls gave out loud screams and fell overboard into the water.

Loss at once sprang on the thwarts with his back to us, he threw off his sou'wester, shot out his arms, poised himself a second or two and then went into the river with a terrible gutser. There was a lot of spray rising from the water beyond the boat, we could see it splashing up as though a tremendous struggle was going on, but as the boat drifted on down we saw three figures rising into view dripping wet, they were standing in a line on the sandbank in the middle of the river, almost up to their knees in water.

We saw Loss getting the water out of his eyes and then wading down after the boat. As the two girls climbed back in, soaking wet, the door of the tower behind us flew open and a dark buxom young woman ran out pulling a red jumper on over her head.

"Carl, Carl," she shouted, in a very posh English voice. "Carl, are you all right, darling, are you all right ?" She ran like mad to the end of the jetty, taking no notice at all of Gronow and me.

Gronow looked inflated, although he was standing still his flesh seemed to be convulsed, it was making those jerky swelling leaps you see in the curtains when there's a breezy window open behind them. "Saint Christopher," he hooted, pointing out at Loss. "Saint Christopher, induced by a blow on the head with a bottle. The Christophero Sly of the mountains." He went his length on the rocks at the foot of the cliff and lay there in uproar.

The young woman in the red jumper heard him, she turned and shook her fist fiercely in our direction.

RHYSIE AT AUNTIE KEZIA'S

I had noticed a lot of whispering in our house that Christmas and there was something the matter with our Mam. But I didn't know what it was. Then one night, when he was finishing his bath by the fire, Dada said to me, "Evan, you are going to your Auntie Kezia's for a bit tomorrow. Over Christmas. Your Mam isn't very well. You see you behave yourself, now."

"Is our Rhysie coming ?" I asked him at once.

My father's head was coming through his flannel shirt just as I said it, and he shook it very slowly without saying a word. There was a very cunning sort of expression on his face.

Still, it wasn't bad in my Auntie Kezia's out there in the country. Sometimes you would find a square of thick grass growing under the bed in her cottage, and every time the trains passed by, her piano played by itself, the keys tinkled a little tune from one end to the other.

Early the next morning Mrs. Richards next-door took me to the station with my little cardboard week-end case in my hand. It had been snowing a lot in the night and the gatepost outside our house had been given a white brow and a big snout. As I looked back at the house from the pavement I could see two or three of my little sisters waving goodbye in the parlour window, but my brother Rhysie was still upstairs, I could see him up there in his nightshirt, his big ugly face pressed against the attic window scowling down at me. He couldn't come down to see me off because my father had hidden his shirt and trousers before he went to work, he didn't trust Rhysie and he wanted to make sure he wouldn't dodge out and come to my auntie's with me.

Mrs. Richards hurried me up town to the station but the snow was thick in the streets and we didn't get on to the platform until the guard was getting his whistle out and his green flag unrolled ready. I got into a compartment at the back end of the train and then, just as our neighbour was saying goodbye to me, I spotted a funny-looking girl running down the empty platform towards us, she was in a big hurry, limping and waving her coat about above her head and shouting at the top of her voice. As she came nearer I recognised her. It was our Rhysie. He had gone down into the girls' bedroom, I could see that, and he was wearing a white satin party dress with ribbons belonging to our Mari, sleeveless, too tight for him everywhere, and on his feet he had our Mam's lace-up boots with the high heels. He had put a couple of bangles on his bare arms too and on his head was Gwennie's big pink sunbonnet tied under his chin with the ribbons.

Mrs. Richards didn't know what to do. Rhysie jumped into the compartment and before she could make up her mind the guard blew his whistle and waved his flag and the train started off. As he sat opposite me, scowling as usual, his bare arms and his face purple with cold, I had to admit he looked a pretty ugly sight ; his upper lip was thick and long, it bulged out over his teeth as though he had his tongue always stuffed under it, and he had the biggest nose of any boy I have ever seen, bent and bony and twisted on one side, and always very red and sore-looking. Anyway, when our auntie met us at the other end and saw that tough-looking face glaring up at her from under the sunbonnet, I thought she was going to have a turn.

Nobody who knew Rhysie seemed to trust him, and that night we had to sleep in the same room as our auntie. She had hung a white bed-sheet across the middle and we could see her shadow undressing on it by the light of her candle. In the morning Rhysie woke up first and because he didn't have anything to do he started to cut my hair with our auntie's scissors. He had a row for that when he got into the kitchen but he was used to it.

Our auntie put him into the spare clothes my mother had packed for me in my cardboard case and bundled us both off to school in the village. Everything was still thick with snow, the scene on the way was pretty, but we were cold. The school was small with only two teachers, and the headmaster was giving the children their Christmas examination. He was a very thick short man with little arms and legs, and over his big bald head he had a few tails of wavy bright yellow hair like flat unravelled rope. Rhysie and I sat in the same desk in the front row and he asked us questions about Saint Nicholas in a big voice. We couldn't answer any of them but he didn't give us a row. Instead he started to sing "While shepherds watched" loud enough to deafen you, banging like mad on the school piano at the same time. When he finished all the children clapped.

In the playground a boy called Bazzo shouted, "Dunce" after Rhysie. Rhysie punched him in the chest and the ribs and clipped him across the side of the head. The boy tried to kick him on the thigh and Rhysie closed with him. They fell to the ground struggling and rolling about in the wet snow and soon the boy began to cry because Rhysie was beating him. When I pulled Rhysie off there were two purple sets of teeth marks in his cheeks, perfect, where Bazzo had bitten him twice. That night after tea, when our auntie was doing a bit of extra washing, a woman called at the back door and complained that Rhysie had nearly murdered her boy. Auntie Kezia believed her and Rhysie went to bed without any supper.

Rhysie didn't like exams so the next day he got me to mich. We went down the main road and spent our time throwing snowballs at the white stone-ginger bottles holding the wires on the telegraph poles. There were stones inside the snowballs. That night Pugh the policeman called in at our auntie's about it and she began to look more worried than ever. She was a small woman, her face yellow as a canary, and she had pale blue eyes always swimming about in a lot of water, she looked as though her eyeballs were slowly dissolving with anxiety.

Rhysie and I didn't like this Pugh at all. He was the shortest policeman we had ever seen, and the fattest, and he couldn't see properly without his glasses. If you watched him from the side standing on the front doorstep in his street you would notice that a lot of him was hanging out over the pavement. He had a big curving moustache and a red face the colour of an old roof, with the nose-part varnished, and half a dozen bottom teeth that stood up brown and rotten like a few old clay pipes in the fair ground shooting gallery. He was very bossy and if he saw you kicking your cap up the street he would shout at you to stop it. And even if the village people left their ash-boxes outside a bit too long in the morning he would knock at the door and tell them to take them in.

The third day was the Christmas party in the church vestry for the village children. Rhysie coaxed our auntie to let us go, although I didn't want to much because of the mess Rhysie had made of my hair. The vestry was a very small low building built all of dark brown wood. For the party it was decorated with streamers and balloons, and crowds of kids from the village were screaming and running about the place in their best clothes. Rhysie and I had a good tea by ourselves after all the others had finished and as we were eating it a tall man came and talked to us. We thought he must be the vicar. His thick loaf-coloured hair was parted deep down the middle, it looked like the cut in a crust of bread. He asked us who we were and when we told him he shot up one of his eyebrows into his hair, pulled it down quickly, and then went away.

After tea all the gaslights in the vestry were turned out and the place was in darkness except for the little candles alight on the Christmas tree. The vicar told us all to be quiet and to look up at the roof at the place he was pointing to, just above the tree. We saw the wooden manhole in the ceiling taken away and a face, with glasses on and a big white beard, showed in the square hole, looking down at us. It was Santa Claus. A ladder was fetched and after a big struggle he began to climb down into the vestry in his hood and his red robes. Some of the little children screamed when they saw him, but Rhysie and I knew him by his boots and his big bum, we could see it was old Pugh the policeman.

Pugh stood short and fat in his red gown and his wadding beard by the Christmas tree and after blowing a bit he started to unhook the presents off it and give them to the children. I was standing in the crowd with my elbow against Rhysie's jersey and the funny thing was I could feel his chest bumping like mad with excitement. I suppose he had set his mind on something on that tree, a knife with a spiker was what he liked, or a box of caps for his cowboy gun or a mouth organ. But by the time the gases were lit again everybody had a present except Rhysie and me. I suppose they forgot about us because we didn't live there.

While the children were laughing and shouting and running about the vestry with their presents Pugh suddenly called us all around him again, we had to stop whatever we were doing and listen to him. He pushed back his hood, unhooked his beard off his moustache and gave us all a good row. It would be the worst for us if any of us went into the graveyard to play snowballs, he told us, looking over his glasses. We could look out, or he'd give us snowballs. The children went very quiet, and after that we all got our clothes and went home.

The next day was Sunday and I knew Rhysie was up to something but he didn't tell me what it was. He couldn't come to church again after tea, he said, because the shaking of the organ had given him the bellyache in the morning. But when our auntie and I got home after the evening service we couldn't find him in the cottage. I thought perhaps he had gone to meet us and had missed us in the dark so I went back towards the church to look for him by myself. When I got to the church lane somebody called me in a whisper and I found Rhysie hiding in the hedge. He wanted me to go and play snowballs in the graveyard.

"Don't be so dull," I said. "You know what old Pugh said last night. He'd screw us."

"Him ?" said Rhysie. "Old Pugh ? Come on, I'll show you something."

We went over the stone stile into the snow-covered church-yard and started dodging about among the graves, pelting each other with snowballs. Every time I hit him Rhysie let out a loud yell. I couldn't make out what had come over him, he seemed as though he had gone daft.

All of a sudden he stopped shying and said, "Look out, here he comes."

We dodged behind a big grave-stone and twtied down there out of sight. In a minute the moon came out full again and I could see Rhysie had a candle there in a jamjar and a white nightshirt, it looked to me like one of our auntie's. He got a box of matches out of his pocket and lit the candle. He slipped the nightshirt on, but the neck part had been tied so that it wouldn't come over his head. "What are you going to do, our Rhysie ?" I asked him, but he didn't answer.

As we crouched in the snow we could hear somebody climbing over the stone stile, coming into the graveyard with a lot of noise.

"That's him," Rhysie whispered from inside the shirt. "It's Pugh. I saw the back door of his house opening just now. Listen to this."

He let out a loud moan.

"Who's there ?" Pugh shouted. "Drat you, I'll give you playing snowballs in the graveyard. Who's there ?"

Rhysie waited a bit and then moaned again, louder this time but more creepy. Pugh seemed to be hesitating near the stile but in a minute we heard him crunching slowly up the path in the snow.

"Who's there ?" he said again, trying to sound brave. "Who's there ?"

I peeped out from behind our stone. There he was, fat and short, not twenty yards away down the path, holding on to a headstone. The moonlight was strong and I could see everything about him, his shiny buttons and the badge on his helmet and his big moustache. But he didn't have his glasses on. That was a funny thing.

Rhysie moaned the third time and as he did it the moon suddenly backed into the clouds and the whole graveyard went black as pitch. In the darkness Rhysie slipped on to the flat tombstone behind us, I saw him kneeling upright on it, his head was gone, he was glowing like a huge gas-mantle, holding the nightshirt away from his body with the candle in the jamjar under it.

There was another loud moan, but Rhysie didn't make it. I looked out at Pugh clutching at the headstone. He wasn't there. I looked again. He was splodged down on the snow, spread out on the path, tipped out helpless as a cart-load of mortar. He had fainted.

We left everything and ran home to our auntie, terrified out of our lives. Rhysie began to cry.

The next day she sent us packing. But we had been away just long enough. When we got home we had a new little brother and our Mam had named him Christmas.

LIAS LEWIS

The forest glowed like a forge in the setting sun as the unbrushed and dilapidated remains of a fat man walked his three geese among the trees.

The man's name was Lias Lewis, and his tall gaunt body moved through the sunset beams in a greenish-black jacket that fell in grooves about his bony figure, and a shabby pair of greenish-black trousers with a hanging seat. The only place where he carried any weight now was in his heavy nose, and that shot out broad and purple from the wanness of his face with the bulky curve of a waterfall. He had bushy eyebrows, pure white eyeballs, and a beard of two reds.

As Lias saw the radiant trees prowling round him, silent and incandescent, he recalled with pride the blazing bush and Nebo's patriarchal bones, he thought of unburied Enoch, the seventh from Adam, and of that Baal-baiting, bullock-burning Tishbite whose name he bore. In that golden afterflush, remembering the miraculous uprapping into paradise of prophets who had never tasted death, he thumped the forest grass with his thumbstick again and again, and cried aloud in rapture like the holy jumpers ; his blazing white eyes sent their powerful glare even through the skin of his shut lids at the thought of the whirlwind, and the flaring stallions, and the Israelitish charioteers.

Then, with the roar and the red-hot glow of a sky-bound angel, Lias himself went thunder-bolting up through the forest branches, hearing ahead the thrilling roll of majestic thunder, the deafening welcome of silver trumpets and of tenor drums ; as he trailed the flames of his whirl-blast over the village house-tiles and the chimney-pots, he saw Rachie Pritchard gazing upwards, dumb with alarm on her dirty doorstep ; and the staring horse-teeth of Maesypiod prominent in the open cut of his mouth ; there beneath him he caught a glimpse of the dyed hair of Cadi Bryncoed, and of Lonso drunk at the roadside, with his head lolling half-way down his spine. And further on in the sawcut of the village street he could see a howling swarm of children, and on the red road Maddox the Minister, the unfaithful, the servant-souled, beetling his way with his little basket to visit the sick after evening chapel.

Lias opened his eyes suddenly on geese and grass and glowing timber, he groaned aloud and banged his thumbstick on the path, because he was back on earth again among the thieves, and the trulls, and the blasphemers of Pwllybaw.

*   *   *

It was a Thursday as the gaunt and dusty old man dreamed of his apotheosis, the night of the prayer-meeting, but all chapel was soup without salt to Lias now. He bitterly remembered his last visit a few weeks ago, and, "Shame, shame," he muttered to himself at the recollection of it. Maddox the Minister had raised the text that Sunday out of the book of Jonah, holding up in his *hwyl* his short arms that didn't reach above the top of his head, preaching the prophet was swallowed, not by the whale, but by Babylon the Great City. Lias went into a ferment at the words. His head glowed like an oven, he felt his heart thundering against the hollow back of the pew, and his blood beat so hard in his feet that his tight best boots tapped out loud like clocks. And this was not the first time ; Lias remembered the preacher saying Elias his namesake was fed by the *natives* beside Kerith, and the word *ravens* was somebody's mistake.

After the meeting he ran home through the darkened village in a fever of resentment and offended pride, banging his bony head as he ran. All Sunday night he groaned in a frenzy, wrestling on the bed with Maddox the Minister, forgetting to lock up the geese and water the shorthorn. At daybreak he was on the preacher's doorstep with his massive brass-bound Bible opened across his chest at the book of Jonah. But it was no use, no use, however adamant was Lias and zealous for the belly of the whale.

"Lias *bach*," said Maddox still in his nightshirt, his white teeth chattering inside the doorway, "if you want to believe Jonah went into the creature, you believe it."

"If I want to believe it !" said Lias, feeling the furnace again and the pumping blood. "Why shouldn't I believe it ? If it said it here I would believe the whole ship went into the creature and came out again the other end without striking a sail."

He left raving. Sunday or week-night, he would never frequent the meeting again.

*   *   *

And yet during those few weeks he had already begun to feel homesick for chapel, for the clean reek of the oilcloth on the aisles on a warm summer's morning, and the sound of the varnished woodwork of the pews creaking in the stillness with a sticky crack as the people sat down heavily in them and prayed.

But these thoughts were vanity, his pride hounded them back into the corner, remembering hungry-for-money Maesypiod with a lot of neck at the back of his head, sucking during communion the sacramental wine through his teeth like a thirsty horse ; and black browed Cadi Bryncoed who never gave an egg to the cause in her life, bulging in her print frock and heaving the flowery garden of her back as she howled the hymns. The dregs. Between them and their potch. He was proud he had no more to do with them. He was better than any of them if they would only see it. How many of them would have sold their only milker as he had done, and she suffering from udder-warts, because she haunted the darkness every time he closed his eyes to meditate on the wickedness of Pwllybaw ? How many of them, although he was everywhere known as one lazy to wrath, would have used the lump-hammer on the neighbour who tempted him to drop a pill into the ailing sow on the Sabbath ? How many would have taken his own wife's gold and silver, her chest-chain, her sinful brooches, her devil's earrings, and handed them all over to his sister ?

At the remembrance of these things a scalding blush of pride spread over his whole head, and to cool it he took off his plaid cap with the tied-up ear-flaps. The skull of Lias was brown and very bald, it had a knobbly ridge running the length of it as though his backbone was coming up over the top of his head.

*   *   *

On his way back home Lias trod the high path above the sunken road that ran through the forest. His three white geese as he walked plucked at the gay green mane of the grasses, and above his head the silent evening sky, blue and clear, was lit with long frills of sunset fire.

Hearing a footstep on the road below him he peeped through the trees down into the cutting, and saw a short plump man dressed in black walking lightly along the red road. It was Maddox the Minister, a man with a large bare head, powerful glasses, and cheerful rosy cheeks, carrying his black hat on top of his little basket. As he passed along below, underneath the pale eyes of Lias, the old man saw the preacher's stiff black hair sticking out round his scalp like a bird's nest, and the large white egg of his bald-spot laid in the middle of it.

Lias glared down in scorn. The minister stopped on the road right below him and began to nod his head in time as a little tune tinkled into the evening silence ; nod, nod, went his head, as the delicate little melody, sweet and clear as a peal of tiny bells, floated up to Lias out of the sunken road. The old man frowned, puzzled and angry, before he knew the music came from the little clock chiming under the black hat in the little preacher's basket. He shook his fist as the tune stopped and the minister moved on again, he shook his fist again and again in outraged dignity at the thought of this clock-cleaning minister, until the small big-headed figure had disappeared joyfully round the bend. Then, beating the grass with his thumbstick, he started his way angrily for home.

*   *   *

Farther on Lias himself entered the sunken road where the air was dim and the crimson earth of the cutting covered by an exposed basket-work of tree-roots.

All of a sudden Lonso trampled at a slow trot round the bend, with his hulking lurcher following behind him the size of a black pony. He was narrow and shorter than Lias, a blackguard and a poacher, his blaspheming tongue and his unshaved goatskin face made people afraid of him. He was sweating through running. He had been fighting again and he had one eye buried in black. His broken clay, soaked with dribbles, was cackling upside down on the black brink of his crinkled teeth. On his head he had a whole felt hat with a piece of golden thatching-twine going up over the top and under his chin to hold it on. He was wearing wet hobnailed boots, sopping corduroys tied under the knees, and a long black overcoat almost reaching the road, ragged, ticketed all over with fluttering edge-tears and with a new six-inch nail skewered through the middle buttonhole to hold it together. One sleeve of this coat was empty, because years ago, poaching, he had blown his left arm off with a shotgun. His flea-marked neck was bare and Lias could see inside his flannel shirt the dirty string on which he hung his lucky lump of bacon fat.

"The only good I know of this creature," said Lias angrily to himself as Lonso approached, "is this. Once I saw him drive away from outside the chapel vestry those noisy children playing by the river and disturbing the prayer-meeting with their shouting. Now he is hurrying to reach the ' Black Horse ' before the tap is turned off. I have no call to talk to such a blackguard as he is."

Lonso continued his trot until he came right up to Lias. When their clothes were nearly touching he stopped, took his pipe out of his mouth and put it under the armpit of his stump. Then he dived into his inside pocket and brought out a fat fish about ten inches long with a green twig through its gills.

"How much, deacon ?" he said to Lias, sticking up his hairy face. His good eye was pink and fierce, the headstrong eyeball greasy. The dog, a black long-haired lurcher with webbed feet, lay down across the roadway and showed his fangs to the hissing geese.

"I am not a deacon," Lias shouted, the anger powerful within him at the touch and the evil smell of this thief and drunkard, this ragged fish-stinking Ishmael. The thumbstick in his hand seemed to come alive like the rod of Aaron, he wanted to use it as the hairy, animal face pushed up into his own, and the poached fish dangled silver on its willow twig. "Thou shalt not covet and thou shalt not steal." he cried out in temper, trying to push on past the snarling lurcher.

"What about a groat for it ?" asked Lonso grinning, taking no notice of the uproar. "What about one little groat ?"

"A groat will buy a pint of the tavern liquor. Wine is a mocker," Lias shouted again, "strong drink is raging."

Lonso lowered the fish. "Thruppence then," he said. "A thruppenny bit for a twelve ounce sewin."

Lias could feel the anger bursting his boots and thundering under his plaid cap. "I wouldn't give you a penny for it," he bawled back. "Not a penny." But when he moved the lurcher bared his tusks.

"A penny ? Let's cut the apple in half and call it tuppence," Lonso said, wheedling, showing the black of his teeth in a bad-smelling smile.

Lias's eyes filled up with tears of rage. He began to stammer. "I said I would give you nothing for it," he shouted. "Nothing at all."

"You want it for nothing ?" Lonso grumbled. "Are you trying to milk me ? What is the matter with you, Lias ?"

"Lonso," said Lias, sighing loudly, trying to cool down. "The tighter the string the nearer to snapping, so I had better say no more than this now : I don't want the sewin. And for why ? To poach is unlawful. To sell what is stolen is unlawful. And I will not part with silver that you will put into the drawers of the ' Black Horse ' before ten minutes are over."

"Me ?" said Lonso, baring his pink gums. " 'The Black Horse ' ? I'm soaking up to the knees, and I'm going straight home to have my supper."

"I thought," said Lias, "you were sweating to reach the ' Black Horse ' before they stop the tap." Then suddenly an idea ran glittering round inside the old man's skull like a ball of quicksilver. What if he, Lias Lewis, could convert this un-chastened outcast, what if he could subdue the defiance of his corrupted heart and bring him over Jordan contrite and with his flesh healthy ? What if he were seen some Sunday morning by Maddox the Minister and his followers—O, moment sweeter than the suck of honeycomb—walking the village with Lonso and Elisabetta, well-clothed, well-washed, and wed beside him ? What a triumph ovet the saints that would be !

"Lonso," he said softly, "listen to me. When wilt thou and all thy house return to the commonwealth of Israel ? Answer me. When wilt thou marry Elisabetta and step within the circle of the promise ? Through the windows of Ramah I saw thee during the meeting, one working-night, driving away the noisy imps who played *talu pump* by the river outside the chapel and disturbed our meditations. Thou showedst there, Lonso, thou hadst reverence for the sanctuary. When wilt thou leave the wilderness and like Joshua possess the land ?"

Lonso's pink eye blazed, he laughed, showing the charred stumps stuck round his salmon gums. A powerful fish-and-stable stink surged up to Lias off him. "Why don't you try washing the feet of the ducks," he said, pocketing the fish, "instead of preaching to me ? Do you know why I put my finger in the chapel broth and drove the children away ? I had spotted a ten pound salmon under the river bank further down the water and I was afraid the children would disturb it with their riot. When they were all gone I landed it and Dafis gave me a dozen pints for it in the ' Black Horse.' Good-night now, Lias. If Elisabetta hasn't got my supper ready I'll break her arm. And if she has I won't eat it. Come on, Fan," he said, and the two of them trampled on down the road, Lonso with his pipe-smoke hurdling his shoulder and his empty coat-sleeve blowing back behind him.

*　　　*　　　*

The sun was almost setting as Lias and his three geese skirted the edge of the huge open field in the middle of the forest. The last low beams thrust themselves in between the trunks of the beech trees and lay in bright yellow stripes across the path like light issuing from many half-opened doors.

Two cottages, grimily limed and dilapidated, squatted close together before him, and the more sluttish one belonged to Rachie Pritchard. He could see her zinc roof tarred and white-washed in broad stripes, and her two long chimney-pots like a stiff pair of khaki trouser-legs sticking up into the air through her roof. Across the window, with two tomatoes ripening in it, hung a square of lace curtain sagging with dust, and the bottom of her front door was repaired with pieces of soiled unpainted timber, shaped like the teeth of a gigantic saw. On the doorstep stood a tipped dish of grey dog-slop and there were peelings and ashes in the large pools of muddy grey water before her door.

"Poor Matthew," said Lias as he approached, thinking of Rachie's little husband, and of Rachie herself, with her body like the parish stallion. "Poor Matthew," he said, "he went through the wood and picked up a rotten branch."

People said Matthew had to keep his dog in the bedroom to save himself from Rachie. And once when she had emptied the teapot out through the front door she saw a little crowd of the village children searching among the tea-leaves. She stood puzzled on the doorstep for a minute, and then she shouted, "Children, what are you looking for?" "Only to see, Rachie," they answered, running away, "if you have thrown Matthew out with the tea-leaves."

But Matthew had been separated from her since then, and now he was living in the other cottage next door. And Rachie by this time was going wild as a bullock after the big-bodied roadman with the hook hand.

O to be delivered from the iniquity of this village, O to rise blazing on angelic wings as on that whirlwind of revenge that once blew all the cabbages out of the ground, O to be tied as it were to the tail of a shooting star, leaving behind all those village brats bold enough to have called Elisha bald-head, and the fornicators bedded behind blackberries, and the fish-poachers and the lewd adulterers, the swill-bellies and the beer-bibbers, and Maddox the Minister the blasphemer, the setter-forth of strange gods, and the servant of all.

Lias drove the three geese in anger past Rachie's rag-spread hedge, which had a lot of bottles flung into it, and a rusty rat-trap, and a tin enamel plate.

But before he reached the cottages themselves he stopped. Matthew, he knew, was off somewhere, away in the next parish burying his mother, but somebody was picking fruit in his

apple tree. As Lias watched, he saw the heavy aproned body
of Rachie beginning laboriously to descend the ladder out of
the branches. She had fat legs bulging over her ankles, she
looked as though she had a pair of leggings on under her black
woollen stockings. In the middle of her face there was a large
oval depression where her mouth and her eyes were set and out
of the middle of which rose two soft red nostrils and a flattened
shapeless nose, pale like the underside of a strawberry where
the little green seeds grow in it. Seeing Lias approaching she
grinned, showing in her wide open mouth her jaws packed with
crowds of unweeded little teeth.

"Lias," she shouted, as common as grass, "come here, come
here. Like to buy a few of these apples ? Eaters ! Draw water
from your teeth !"

Lias felt many words to denounce her thieving and her
adulteries rising within him, and a deep religious flush, purple
in colour, heating his face. But what was the use of rebuking
her ? The more you tread on mud the muddier it gets. After
his talk with Lonso he would more than ever use his teeth to
hold his tongue and go by without answering.

"Look at these indeed, Lias," she shouted from the ladder,
showing him Matthew's rosy apples in her apron as he came
on without a word. "It would benefit you to put a few of these
down you. They will wet the root of you tongue. What's
the matter with you, Lias ?" she shouted, seeing him so close
there on the path and still not opening his mouth. "There's
proud you are. Why don't you answer ? Can't you understand
Welsh any more ? Or are you too big to talk because you go
to the satin chapel ?"

Lias felt his flush thicken. She was laughing at him and the
words of denunciation boiled up into his mouth. But it is
wiser to shelter from a shower than try to stop it, so he hurried
the geese towards her. Soon he would be past her, and past
the apple tree, and the whole of her garden and Matthew's
next door would be behind him.

"Old Lias Lewis," she jeered as he came opposite her in
silence, "the front horse of the satin chapel and a power on his
knees." Every time she shouted a word the fat cushion of her
belly gave a kick upwards jerking up her clothes, and all the

time her eyes glittered at him like hanging drops of water. "Don't you be dull, Lias *bach*," she went on, changing her tone a bit, "you jack that old chapel up and enjoy yourself instead. What are you starving yourself to death for ? Are you so eager to bang the golden harp ? By the look of you another two clean shirts will see you out, and when you are in your box there won't be a wheel the less on the road, remember. Have a bit of fun, boy, and taste a cut of the whitemeat now and then. What odds that you are sixty—there's many a good tune to be had from an old fiddle. Why don't you try wetting your beak for a change ? And have you thought of courting Cadi Bryncoed ? She would be a good one for you—if she hadn't dipped her head in the tar bucket. Let it out, let it out, Lias *bach*, and don't churn it round inside you. Why don't you answer ? Have you got a thick tongue or what ? All right, don't listen, have it your own way ; no fools no fun is what I think. No, I won't throw my slops against the wind for you. You'll be old before I talk to you again, Lias Lewis. Go on, go on, they say the back is the best of the goose. And eat a bit more of food when you get home and then you won't have room for a loaf of bread in the seat of your trousers."

The words drenched heavily over Lias's back like rain before the wind, but at last he was out of hearing. O, the Jezebel, to tempt and despise him. O earthy, sensual and devilish. Would that she could be cast down there among her whorish poppies, to be devoured by the dogs and only her palms and footsoles left uneaten.

Then, just at that moment, as Lias came out into the field from a gap in the hedge, he saw ahead of him at the top of the grassy slope the shining dead tree that stood before his house. It had lost nearly all its bark, and in the last blazing beams of the setting sun its weather-polished trunk and branches gleamed as though they were made, not of white timber, but of pure silvery metal, brightly burnished and massive and solid. Lias stopped to look at it. Was this a portent, was this tree of glowing silver, burning and unconsumed, a sign ? Were these the blazing branches from which he was to take fire and launch himself in splendour over Pwllybaw ? O to be justified, O to be exalted thus in righteousness above Maesypiod and Cadi Bryncoed, and Maddox the Minister, and all the false saints of Ramah. Until that should happen, Lias said to himself, he would swallow his existence and find it tasteless, he would gulp down his unprofitable life ravenously, like a dog with the worms.

*   *   *

Lias stood upright at the top of his dead tree, waiting for the moon to rise. Darkness, lit only by a few diminished stars, was everywhere about him, and from the choral forest below surged up the sound of the baffled winds boiling among the boughs. This was the night for which he had waited, starved himself and importuned providence ; at the uprising of the moon this gusty wind should waft his fleshless body in terrorising circulations over Pwllybaw.

"I will show them," he muttered to himself, smoothing the six goosewings before him. "At last I will show them."

These wings, chopped from the shoulders of his own slaughtered geese, he had nailed fast in a row to the flat of an old swingle-tree, and as the full moon climbed up the darkness he would launch himself upon them like a new Elias and, with denunciations, circle the chimney-pots of the village. "I will show them," he muttered again, "I will show them, every one."

On his high swaying perch he waited. To lighten himself he wore no boots and his long bony body was clad only in a white flannel nightshirt. On his head he had his cloth cap with the flaps tied down over his ears. The wind streamed his beard out from his face like a two coloured flag, and although the chilling winds blew round his body, ballooning his baggy nightshirt, he did not notice the cold. Watching alone in the tall black air he felt fulfilled and exalted. As he gazed up at the black sky, stretched out and glittering like a frosty cloth with stars, his flesh blew out and was magnified again and again, his body seemed to multiply itself, extending towards those distant glimmerings above him. And expanding downwards at the same time it engulfed the massive boniness of the dead tree, the rigid branches seemed completely enveloped within him like the refleshing of a gigantic skeleton. But yet he swayed, he was still light as a breastfeather, the towering fabric of his bulk felt through its airy cells and interstices the cold flow of the night air. O to be among the mighty, O to rise, to float, a holy migrant, through the encompassing firmament, O to be majestic swan or paradisal firebird.

As Lias rocked gently to and fro he lost himself in this forgetful ecstasy, the passage of time increased in speed like a gale around him. Suddenly, without any warning, the whole moon rushed lit into the sky, flinging the shining paint of her illumination over all the sheeted roofs of the village below. Lias's gaze swept up towards the salt glitter of the stars with a prayer for his exaltation, and then, the swingle-tree clasped tightly across his breast, he dived off the dead branches in the direction of Pwllybaw.

*   *   *

Tack-tick, tack-tick, tack-tick, tack-tick.

A lantern was hanging from a hook in the rafters of a small square barn. Beneath it, in the yellow light, Maddox the Minister, his chopped hair sticking out all round his head like untidy twigs, was sitting on an upturned wooden bucket, and unconscious on a thick bed of hay before him, under a covering of sacks, lay Lias Lewis. There were rings in the thick glass of the minister's spectacles, and from his rosy grin was thrust his outstanding china tooth with the corner chipped off. The clothes covering his plump body were all black, and his black hat and hymn-book lay on top of the clock in the basket beside him.

Tack-tick, tack-tick, tack-tick, tack-tick, went the little clock.

There was perfect silence in the barn but for breathing and clock-ticks, and then Rachie Pritchard, weeping as she knelt in the hay at the minister's feet, started to whisper in an empty-chapel voice. "I was sitting down in the kitchen," she whimpered, "when I heard an awful scream—as though somebody had a knife at his throat. I went weak at the knees, but you will have to tie me up to stop me, Mr. Maddox, when somebody is wanting my help, so I put my foot to the earth . . ."

"Poetry, poetry, Rachie Pritchard," said Lonso, cross and

in low tones. "I love her sort like a row of neckboils," he growled to the minister. "Bragging, always bragging, sir." He was kneeling the other side of Lias from Rachie and in his hat and mangy overcoat he stank like a dead horse.

"You leave me alone, Lonso," Rachie answered, using her flannel apron on her scooped-out face. "I'm big enough to say my piece myself I am."

"The cow is big enough to catch the rabbit," he said, "but nobody has ever seen her doing it. I was going for a walk in the moonlight, Mr. Maddox, sir," he whispered, saluting his tied-on hat, "when I heard that scream. I ran to the roots of the dead tree, and there I found the old man lying on the grass, groaning, with his leg folded in half under him and his ripped nightshirt wrapped round his head. I straightened him out and when Rachie came we got him in here. That's the middle and both ends of it, sir."

He looked down. "I must drink more of water," he thought to himself. "I must from now on. Bull's beer. Better for me than swilling bottle-ale. What if I was to die like Lias ? Poor old dab," he went on aloud, "he looks to me, Mr. Maddox, as though he is knocking at the gate already."

The gaunt and broken body of Lias lay outstretched between him and Rachie, dressed in his cap and rumpled nightshirt still. They had made the thick bed of hay under him and piled the sacks on his body to keep him warm. His leg was broken, his face torn, and tears were tearing out of his lids and along his cheeks, making for his red beard. While the three gazed down he bared his marble eyeballs. "Pray for me, Mr. Maddox," he whimpered feebly, "pray for me. I have fallen, somebody is thumping me on the head, and I have cut the forehead of my knee." Then closing his eyes again he clasped his hands upon his chest in readiness for prayer. They were thin and hairy, like a heavy crop of red hairs growing on bare bones.

"Yes, yes, I will pray for you, Lias," the rosy minister answered. "But tell us how it happened, Lias *bach*. Tell us how it happened."

Tack-tick, tack-tick, tack-tick, tack-tick went the unseen clock as the old man rocked his head on the hay from side to side. But at last he opened his eyes again and spoke between the sobs.

"I fell out of the tree, Mr. Maddox," he said, "I fell out of the tree. In my pride I climbed up into the tree, and I had my fall. The goose-wings were powerless, my nightgown opened like an umbrella and tipped me upside down." He groaned in remembrance, and hearing him Rachie sobbed to herself. "I must chase the dust in that parlour tomorrow," she muttered. "What if I died like poor Lias ?"

"Through a rip in my nightshirt," Lias went on, "I could see the blinding moon going bump, bump, bump, it was wheeled round the horizon on a broken-wheeled wheelbarrow. The next thing I knew was I opened my eyes on the dung-fork and the wooden rake there in the corner. I am black," he cried aloud in anguish, "I am black, black, and my pride has killed me. In my pride I sold the shorthorn and the golden chains, in my pride I abandoned the chapel of my fathers. In my pride I climbed the tree and prayed to be exalted above my neighbours. I shall never be forgiven, never, never, and I will now draw in my feet and die."

He looked tearfully up at the minister. His swollen nose was black and soft, pulpy, like a lump of burning wool bubbling on the fire, and his scratched face had turned colour as though he were blushing green.

"No, no, Lias," said the minister, "repentance, repentance. Have you forgotten about repentance ? God is good, remember."

Rachie bent over the old man, weeping, her greasy bobbed hair hanging out of her head like leather laces. "I must give up courting that Roberts the roadman too," she was thinking. "That's right, Lias," she whispered, showing her unthinned crop of teeth in a crying grin. "Raise your heart, raise your heart, boy. God is good, and the devil is not so bad." She looked up at the minister for encouragement, with massive tears bulging out of her eyes. "It breaks my heart to see him so low in his spirits, Mr. Maddox," she said. "I'll take this tight old cap off, for him to have his agony out in comfort." As she sat on the hay her nose was scarlet with weeping, and her stockings were so fat she looked as though she had her feet on the wrong legs.

The old man groaned aloud as she bared the battered

backbone running the length of his bald head, he cried out as though he were giving up the ghost.

"Every one of us needs forgiveness, Lias," said the minister. "Evil is the portion of all flesh, our iniquities and transgressions are manifold and numbered with the morning dew. You answer him too, Rachie. And you, Lonso. Why don't you answer him ?"

"I don't know, Mr. Maddox, sir," said Lonso, "I don't know about forgiveness, sir, myself. But I won't argue with you, sir. I know my weight. I must give up that poaching," he was thinking. "No if-and-half about it, I must give it up altogether. What if I died like Lias Lewis ?"

"Don't know indeed," said Rachie, wiping her cheeks and glaring at Lonso. "Ask him, Mr. Maddox, what he was doing out in the field tonight. Him going for a walk in the moonlight !"

Lonso glared back across at her in one-eyed resentment. "You stop your blowing, Rachie," he growled.

"Going to see his night-lines, that's what he was doing," she said. "He's always poaching. Going for a walk indeed ! And he's swaying every day by dinner time when he can afford it. And what about that Elizabetta he's living with ?" She folded her bare fat arms in defiance but she was so stout they would hardly meet over her bosom.

Lonso shook his stump in her face across the groaning old man. "She's on my back every chance she gets. And only tonight I saw Roberts the roadman coming out of her garden. What did he call to see you for at nearly midnight, Rachie ?" he jeered. "Was it to show you the muscles of his back ?"

Rachie coloured and tears began to pour out of her again. She buried her face in her hands, and as her man-shaped shoulders shook with weeping, the water sprang out between her fingers. For a moment there was silence in the room. Then the minister spoke quietly with a grin on his face.

"You see, Lias *bach*," he said, "we are all, every one of us, in need of forgiveness."

Lonso glared and then he too dropped his head.

"Let us do what Lias asks us," Maddox went on. "Let us have a little prayer. Lonso, take your hat off, if you please."

"I know my manners, Mr. Maddox, sir," Lonso muttered, talking down into the neck of his shirt. "I was raised on the breast of religion." He pulled off the golden string round his hat, and his head was thick with fur like a thatched roof ; it sloped up sharply from above his ears like the roof of a house with grass sides. Lonso, holding his hat under his arm-stump, Rachie, fingering her wet apron, and Maddox the Minister, the yellow lamp-light like a halo in his hair, knelt down around the hay bed of Lias, and the minister prayed for grace and the forgiveness of sins.

"Blessed is forgiveness," he said, "blessed is the clean day-star of repentance after the night, and the dawn of innocence like the rising of the sun. Then to the sinless heart is the world renewed, the trees of the field shout and wave their green arms, the bright waters shout, branchy among the rocks of the river. The small flowers of the grasses burst open in the sun, and every moment a wave of perfume leaves the earth. The little roof-birds twitter in gladness, the blackbird sings a sweet song, he sings to his Maker a song of praise. Then is the contrite soul exalted, it floats over the dewy fields with the sun of forgiveness smoothing its wings. O to see the night slouch from our hearts and the dayspring of forgiveness shine upon us. Amen."

Tack-tick, tack-tick, tack-tick went the clock, and Rachie and Lonso said their amens in silence. All three opened their eyes and looked down at Lias. He lay pale and quiet among them under the sacking, and the stillness of death was like a light upon him. Seeing that a big hole had opened in his beard where his mouth was, and the hairy bones of his hands were still clasped immovably upon his breast, the eyes of the three signalled to each other. The minister nodded and began to get up off his knees.

But suddenly the sacks fell away from Lias as he sat up on the hay. "Amen !" he shouted. "Hallelujah ! How beautiful, how beautiful ! My heart is hot with forgiveness, and in a soft place, it is like putting the frozen hand under the sitting hen. And for why ? At last I am exalted, I am exalted, but in forgiveness, in my forgiveness I shall lead Rachie and Lonso like Israel to repentance."

His blazing, colourless eyes flashed from one to the other, and the two fell back in terror before the prophetic flashings of his beard.

"Rachie," he cried, pointing a bony hand at her, "you put the wool on the pins and begin by forgiving Lonso. And you, Lonso, you take your claws out of Rachie's feathers. You must promise me, Lonso, before I go, you must promise me, Rachie, that you will repent. Promise me and I repose, I am refreshed, I die in peace. Promise me and I am forgiven, on the flat of my deathbed I am forgiven for my pride."

Rachie looked up frightened at the minister, her tears pumping down her cheeks. "Hallelujah," she sobbed, broken-hearted. "Yes, Lias, I know what you mean. I will go back to Matthew tomorrow."

There was silence as a shower of drops hot as candle-grease fell on her bare arm. Then the bushy fire of the beard swung to the other side. "Lonso !" Lias shouted.

"Amen," said Lonso hurriedly, his eye bulging and a look of terror on his hairy face. "Amen," he gulped. "Yes, all right, Lias, I will marry Elisabetta, Lias. I will marry Elisabetta in Ramah, Mr. Maddox, sir, for ever and ever, amen and amen."

Lias smiled, drew his bushy brows down over his eyes and fell back, still, upon the hay.

"He is dead," Rachie and Lonso gasped together.

The minister got up and opened the half-door of the barn to the night. As the sweet air entered, the hidden clock broke out into its delicate little tune, and the clouds, dividing outside in the darkness, showed three bright stars in a row.

RHAMANT DRIST

The moon crossed the windy sky and the large clouds, meeting her, burst out into black smoke at her touch. On the earth below everything was under the deep snowfall. The hill, curving out from below its black cap of pine forest, was cut into gleaming fields of white velvet, and in the village all the houses wore the heavy fall of whiteness.

A child came toiling down the slope from the forest towards the village. His hair was beaten about his face and although he towed nothing behind him he bent forward into the wind as though he were roped to a heavy load. The cottage he saw before him was enchanting in the moonlight. Wild smoke twisted out of its chimney. The thatched roofs between the lattice windows came half-way down the walls, like the flaps of a cap pulled over the ears for warmth, and the straw was thatched again with a thicker thatch of snow. It had a low garden wall in front on which rested a snowy coping smooth as porcelain and each gatepost was surmounted by a little loaf of snow.

But loveliest of all, standing among the shrubs threshing in the wind, was a new snowman. His hat was a flowerpot, his eyes were two corks and he had a broken side-comb for teeth. He smoked a pipe made out of a sliced potato with a skewer stuck into it. Around his neck the children had tied a check duster for a scarf and there was an upright row of cinders intended for buttons down the front of his white overcoat. He had no feet and his hands were in his coat pockets so that he could hold the leg of the cane-brush under his arm.

The child stopped crying, his fears vanished as he gazed at the entrancing figure bright in the moonlit garden. He climbed over the low wall and as he did so he heard the laughter of the children sounding from the cottage. He crept through the shrubs until he came to the casement window, its sill thickly cushioned with the snowfall. The curtain was not closed and through the diamond panes he could see into the brightly lighted room.

There the big fire pushed its bright horns up into the chimney and the ceiling was festooned with many paper chains and bells of coloured glass. Around the sparkling table some boys and girls were eating a little feast, laughing and talking to one another. The child longed to join them, he was filled with joy that this was the house at which he was to claim admittance. He was about to tap at the panes when he saw the mother open the door of the room and enter it smiling ; she took out all the lamps and candles from the table and left the room in darkness so that all the children were rosy in the glow of the firelight. When she came in again she was carrying a large cake decorated with candles, a ring of slender little candles was burning round the edge, some rose-pink, some pale blue and some primrose yellow, each one standing in a little rosette of coloured sugar. The children, waiting in the warm gloom, cried out loud with delight when they saw the cake and the circle of bright and pure flames. "If you please, if you please," they began chanting, holding out their plates towards the mother.

The child no longer thought of drumming upon the window panes. Silently opening the front door he entered the cottage and sat down at the table. The other children talked to him excitedly in the candlelight as though he had been present from the beginning. He was expectant and enchanted, his heart glowed with happiness at their welcome.

Then, as the mother and her yellow-haired girl were preparing to cut the cake, bangs were heard at the door of the room and then a loud voice cursing. All the children became silent at once, they were pale and their eyes large with alarm. The mother, no longer smiling, turned from the table. There was another outburst of thundering at the door and it was pushed roughly open so that the paper festoons hissed loudly and the small pointed flames on the cake candles leaned back in a ring, tugging together at their little wicks, becoming clear and intense.

The child could see dimly at the door an evil-faced man standing with a lantern in his hand. He was short and heavily built, wearing breeches and gaiters and a brass-buttoned coat. He had a large shining head like a new chestnut, it seemed round as a cannon-ball, too heavy to be moved in its cruelty.

There was a patch over one of his eyes and his black teeth were twisted between his great lips. Under his arm he carried a heavy gun.

The little girl clung to her mother as the man trod angrily into the room. He clattered the lantern down on the table among the tea-things and stared around him. There was silence. Then baring his black tusks at the woman he pointed round fiercely at the children.

"Get them out," he shouted, in a voice hoarse with rage. "Get out, get out, all of you," he screamed at the children, "get out I tell you !"

He lifted his gun and brought the butt down with curses again and again on the large cake, smashing the sugar and filling the air with the reek of put-out candles. The children screamed and fled towards the door. The heart of the child was filled with protest. He could see the happiness of the boys and girls ended, he cried in anguish against it and jumped up to hold back the gun of the destroyer. The man crashed him with a sweep of his arm to the floor, he shook off the mother, slanted his heavy gun at the child and took aim. But before he could fire the nimble child had opened the casement window and was once more out in the night. As he dived through the bushes he saw that the snowman had been pushed over and smashed, it lay in broken pieces on the trampled garden.

He regained the road and trudged onward through the darkness. He sobbed with rage and disappointment. Then in his misery a strange sensation began to take possession of him ; he felt as though the days of his childhood and their bitterness were over and that what lay before him was a different grief. He brushed away his last tear, clinging like a spark to his cheek in the moonlight.

*   *   *

Coming suddenly out of the dark cutting along which he had borne his misery, the lover halted and gazed down in wonder at the radiance of the vast plain before him. The big wind had died. The moon no longer hastened across a sky blue with cold, but stood mellow and assured, pouring out unstanched splendour over the world. The scattered stars trembled like a vast nursery of silver blooms. A broad river moved slowly through the snow, curving among the meadows, and its black waters, caught in a dragnet of silver radiance, glittered. At the foot of a distant hill covered with a forest of dark firs, stood a castle, the dark curves of its towers whitened and its walls flecked with the great plumy snowfall.

As he gazed in silent gladness at the radiance and tranquility of the scene at his feet, his heart was soothed and momentarily pacified. Then he heard a pounding sound in the forest close at hand. Poom-poom-poom, poom-poom-poom, on it came, and then out of the black wood broke a line of horsemen bearing torches, they swept out on to the clear slope of the moonlit hill and rode down at a fierce gallop in the direction of the castle, throwing up the snow in showers behind them. The lover saw them galloping away into the distance and plunging into the glittering river, where they flung their torches wildly into the current. Then, when they had reached the thickets on the further bank, snatches of a chorus reached him faintly, and the abrupted note of a horn, as they disappeared among the shadows of the castle. The lover's heart was troubled to its roots, stirred by the pride and glory of what he had seen. The leading rider, the one upon the large black stallion, plunging masterful through the breakers of his own breathing, had been a woman, her hair burning out behind her in a long blaze from her head.

When he looked at the sky again he could see a star, large and jewel-like, standing motionless above the flag of the castle.

*　　　*　　　*

The room of the castle in which he sat was lighted with two crystal chandeliers. It was an oval room, ornate and gilded, furnished with gold and crimson chairs of plush, and decorated settees. A crimson carpet covered the floor, and on the walls, worked with vivid coats of arms, were hangings of crimson velvet. Armfuls of fresh blond roses, relieved with green fronds, filled the porphyry jars on their pedestals. Several large mirrors, with bunches of candles branching from their gilded frames, were fixed to the walls, giving on every side great depth and brightness. A fire with a cat before it burned brightly in a white fireplace of chiselled roses.

A beautiful woman leaned forward to one of the gilded mirrors in the wall, her head on one side and both her jewelled hands fingering the lobe of an ear. The lover rose from his seat and she, seeing his reflection, his straight black brows and small pointed beard, smiled at him with moistened lips and turned towards the room. A faint blush was burning in the pallor of her cheeks.

She was wearing a white satin gown with a full sequined skirt and a bodice from the foam of which rose her gleaming shoulders. Bracelets sparkled at her wrists ; in her ears were jewels and the base of her throat was ablaze with a deep collar of diamonds. As she stood facing the lover the brightness from the hanging lights fell around her pale face and upon her gleaming hair, a flame mastered now into the formality of plait and curl. The edges of her full red lips were sharp, they looked as though they had burst apart with the ripeness of her scarlet mouth. From her body, from the movements of her dress, came off the cool fragrance of lilies.

She held out her hand to him and he led her, humming to herself, over the dumb carpet to her large black piano. Here she sat and began to sing softly, accompanying herself upon the instrument. The lover sat beside her, watching with enchantment the movement of her glittering lips, watching the planes of overhead brilliance falling about her head and shoulders, the light burning upon her flamy hair, smoothing a bright hand over the waterfall of fire. There was a thundering under his throat, his hair stirred involuntarily and his flesh seemed chilled to ice at her beauty and the incommunicable loveliness of her singing.

The black cat, ignoring the lovers, sat calmly before the fire licking his front paw, holding it up rigid to his red tongue and going over it with the delicacy and absorption of a craftsman.

Suddenly the fire slipped sideways and every coal put up its flag of flame. The woman, seeing the cat scurrying out of sight, left her singing and came over to mend it. She bent, coughed uncertainly and straightened herself, with the back of her hand to her mouth. She looked into the mirror and sobbed in alarm. At the same moment a hound somewhere in the castle began to bay loudly as though in terror, tearing in anguish at his heavy chain.

The lover sprang from his chair towards the woman. From the corner of her mouth poured a vivid line of scarlet. Her hand was covered with a glove of blood and the rosy drops were spread out over the front of her gown. He swung her off her feet and bore her still coughing to the settee. Here, muttering and pleading like one demented, he tried with his handkerchief to stop the blood oozing unstanched from her mouth, but he could not. The woman said no word and in a short time her long-lashed lids carried a darkness down her eyes ; but even in her swoon her coughing continued and at every cough the bright red frothy flow increased. The blood was upon her breast, it had patterned the corsage of her gown with a scarlet lace. It was upon everything that had been touched, upon silk and carpet, upon her body and upon the hair and flesh of her lover.

Presently the scarlet hand with which, even during unconsciousness, she had fiercely gripped his sleeve, relaxed, and the long bangled arm fell away. The lover rose from his knees and stared down in stupefaction ; with the perfume of her rising into the air about him a sensation of protest and unbelief took possession of him. To pass for ever, good and beautiful, under the dark lid of the centuries. But there were cries outside the room, the great ban-dog could be heard upright against the door howling in frenzy and beating and scratching on the panels with his paws. The lover bent down again, buried his hands up to his wrists in the collapsed flame of her hair and kissed again and again the bleeding mouth. Then, ignoring the clamour at the door, he made his way out through the curtains on to the snow-covered lawn.

*   *   *

The soldier went laboriously in the snow along the edge of the seacliff. His heart felt old and numb, so shrieked at, scorched, gashed and thundered upon that it seemed incapable again of being stirred to protest or compassion. He thought of his childhood, how he had defied the stroke of the armed destroyer, of his manhood when one glimpse of the flying riders could warm his heart like wine. Now he was old and wasted, haunted with memories, recalling a child kissing the cold cheek of a snowman, recalling a radiant face, spared, unlike his own, the elaborate and hideous make-up of grief.

Over the land lay a chill and pallid mist. Wearily the moon before him bleared and made downwards for the sea.

From the distance came the hollow sound of firing, as though muffled blows were falling on the soft outside surface of the night. Then there was silence, except for the faint splash of the waves below him.

He went on in the direction of the long lonely headland thrusting a great paw out into the misty sea. Then in the narrow pathway he halted. Approaching him over the crest of a rise he saw the light of a lantern. He had no trust in human-kind and his impulse had become always one of avoidance. There, at the side of the path, grew a wind-dwarfed thicket caked with snow and under this he huddled his bones for safety.

Presently nine or ten men came wearily out of the mist, following one another. They also were soldiers, each one dressed in a dark tattered uniform, some with rifles slung over their shoulders. The leader carried a lantern and his head and face were heavily bandaged. The lantern had one pane of red glass, it hung near his ragbound feet, casting a jerked and distorted disc of light upon the snow. The soldiers approached the twisted bush in a profound hush, each one followed the steps of his comrade, absorbed in his own wretchedness, grave, quiet, moving through the moonlight as though under some enchantment of silence. Only one, coming at a little distance behind the others, uttered any sound. He, with the face of a schoolboy, limped on his way, sobbing bitterly to himself. Then, as the tattered and dejected figures were opposite the bush, a large dark bird loomed behind them out of the mist, he came on beset at first by a dreadful silence, but when he was above them he swooped down on rigid wings, he let out screech after screech of fury and malevolence ; he traversed their file from end to end, menacing their heads with his massive wings and releasing upon them the shrieks of an insane hatred. The soldiers scarcely looked up, they went on in dejection and weariness, maintaining their silence, and presently even the light of their lantern was hidden in the mist.

The soldier rose and went on in the direction from which the file had come. A silver-haired star rested over the point of the headland.

* * *

Around the cabin a grove of dead pines rose into the mist, black and picked bare as fishbones. The moon, almost at the point of setting in the sea, looked distorted through the dividing vapours. The soldier knelt in the snow and in his hands were gripped two square iron bars set in a window frame. He had been in time to see an old man lift up his heavy burden from where it lay at the foot of the outside wall of the house, and to see him bear indoors, swaying under its weight, the dead body of his son.

The underground room into which the soldier peered was dim and bare as a cavern. It was lit by a single candle. Fishing nets hung drying from the rafters like enormous cobwebs. A clock with a motionless pendulum was fastened to the dark wall. A few cinders glowed on the hearthstone. In the middle of the cellar stood a table upon which was stretched the naked body of the young man. On this table the solitary candle burned, standing in its grease beside the head of the corpse, and casting its light upon the wild features.

This was a house into which he must gain admittance. As he watched he saw the old man coming very slowly into the cellar, his feet in heavy sea-boots dragging over the bare flags. He placed a large wooden bucket on a chair beside the table and poured water into it from an earthenware stane. He was a very old man, his black jersey rolled up to his elbows showing sun-blackened arms. On his head was a small black knitted skullcap and his white hair came out in a fringe from under it. In his ears were golden ear-rings. The skin of his wrinkled face also, like his arms, was burnt almost black, and against it his hair and his close beard gleamed silvery as cotton-grass in the candle-light.

For a time he stared in silence at the dead body of his son stretched on the table before him. He placed his palms to his cheeks and rocked his head slowly from side to side in weariness. The body was pitiful, black and emaciated, the belly scooped out and the curved bars of the ribs rising up from the table like a cage with the skin pulled tightly over them. The head was shaggy and unkempt, thickly bearded, the black animal-like hair furry on the neck and growing down over the brows into the eyes. The chest was torn with a row of bullet wounds and down the thigh, from hip to knee, a wound divided the flesh almost to the bone. Round the wrist nearest to the window was a broad strap of brass and a few links of a snapped-off chain attached to it hung over the edge of the table.

The father began to wash the body in the candle-light. He did not weep. As he bent over in absorption and gently sponged the blood away from breast and limbs his lips seemed to be making a crooning sound. From head to foot he went over the glistening flesh, cleansing and swilling away the patches and cakings of blood, until the body was clean and dry ; and then, dashing water upon the hair, he divided it with his fingers, taking it back from the eyes and smoothing it into order.

The moon sank and darkness lay over the snow-covered earth. Birds in a bare-headed birch beside the house began to grieve. The cheeks of the soldier had turned to water at the vision of the old man and his shot son but in his heart at the same time he found a strange emotion stirring. He recognised this stirring as hope.

THE GOLDEN PONY

For the moment the child was at peace and in another world and the terrors of the island were forgotten.

The sun shone warm through the thick glass of the lattice window into the small schoolroom where the heads of the children were bowed over their work. The only sound was the dry creak of the teacher's chair. Then a bluebottle on the window diamonds let go his hold and tumbled droning off the panes about the shabby room. The teacher himself, a hot-skinned man with hob-nailed boots and hair like ginger wool, was drowsing in the airless heat with his chair tilted back and his huge hands locked across his belly. He would sometimes, when he had finished writing with them, lay down his things on the front desk where Rhodri sat, and now in the groove were a fresh stick of white chalk and a new red-ink pen, the wooden holder varnished brown.

Rhodri glanced round the desks. The dozen boys and girls who composed the school wrote round him in silence. He pushed the teacher's piece of chalk forward in the groove, so that the broader part, the white disc of its base, approached the domed end of the shining penholder. The sun poured powerfully on to the desk and the chalk emitted in its radiance a strong reflection, a powerful glow of white light beamed out of the flat disc and illuminated the rounded end of the varnished holder. As the child slowly withdrew the chalk back along the groove the shine on the pen was dimmed and as he slid it forward again the varnish lit up and glowed white in the beam of the oncoming radiance. Rhodri continued to slide the white stick slowly to and fro in grave ecstasy.

The sight called up for him the world which he inhabited with the golden pony, and his heart glowed. Whenever he was completely absorbed, whenever his eyes, his ears or his heart were filled and satisfied, he seemed to have fallen beneath the spell of that gentle golden-coated creature to whose world he attributed all loveliness and joy.

He meant to look up to see if the teacher was still drowsing but a thread of gossamer drifting out of the gloom of the schoolroom corner caught his eye ; slowly it writhed from the shadows into the bright sunlight and suddenly hung burning there brilliant as a firework before floating out into the dimness again.

The edges of Rhodri's exercise book seemed hairy in the clear sunlight as a white cat. He picked up the teacher's pen. The nib was still wet with red ink. He placed it vertically on its point right dead centre of the dazzling clean page of his exercise book. There it cast a long clear shadow across the bright blue lines of the page ; and when he tilted it towards him the shadow lengthened, it seemed to become more slender and elegant, the nib tapering into a point of the greatest fineness and delicacy. And the red ink in the slit glowed, both in the nib and in the firm image of its shadow, it burned with a wet ruby brilliance like a bead of scarlet wine. Rhodri was oblivious of everything. Only the pen and its shadow on the dazzling page existed for him, they absorbed his whole being, and the golden naked horse moved round his mind in a glowing ring, casting upon it the radiance of its strange loveliness.

To reassure himself that the varnish of the new pen tasted bitter as his own usually did he placed the end of the holder between his teeth and gently bit it. Small scales of varnish fell with a sharp taste on to his tongue and he wiped them away with the back of his hand. Then he erected the pen again on its nib and continued to slope it this way and that, with his index finger firm on the domed end, watching with complete absorption the altering shape and intensity of the shadow and the jewel-like brilliance of the scarlet bead glowing on the sunlit paper.

And then he stopped. A shadow had fallen on his desk, completely darkening his sunny exercise book. He lifted his eyes, and close before them was the guttered belly of the hot-faced teacher, a bone button and a thick powdering of chalk in every groove of his waistcoat. The other children must all have been watching Rhodri because when he raised up his head and saw the teacher glaring down at him they all began to laugh.

"Leave things alone," shouted the teacher in his harsh voice, and Rhodri felt a stinging blow fall on the side of his head.

*   *   *

The child had come to live in the island at the death of his parents. His grannie had fetched him from the mainland and they had crossed the sea in stormy weather. As they came down the path to the beach his heart was heavy, he could not keep his tears back with loneliness and foreboding. His grannie walked beside him in her torn and shabby cloak muttering to herself. Whenever she kicked against a stick on the path she picked it up and put it under her cloak. The child had never seen her before. She had a wild brown face and her hair was in disorder. Her large flat eyes were staring and pale, they were fixed wide open and silverish in the darkness of her face. She said nothing to the child but muttered endlessly as she trod in sightless absorption along the path.

The air was heavy around them and utterly still, and the clouds over the whole sky had turned smoky with thunder. Above the sea's horizon a great raw patch was spread as though the outer skin of the heavens had been removed and the angry under-flesh laid bare, crimson, the sombre blood heavy behind it. Then a tree shivered and the sudden cold wind raised a fin of dust along the path. The old woman's cloak burst open. The cold lead-like rain began to fall, but she paid no heed to it. The child could see the ferryboat before them, low in the water, loaded down with people returning from the mainland. The two crossed the pebbles and found room in the stern. The people sat round them in silence and dejection expecting the storm, their dogs and their baskets at their feet.

In the gusty rain the whole air turned cold and dark as nightfall. Seabirds flashed sideways through the wind. The boatman was drunk and his face hideous with a purple disease. He wore black oilskins and cursed the people as he pushed the heavy boat off the pebbles. The rain came in oblique gusts as though shooting out sideways from slits in the sky. The island lay smouldering in the distance, charred and sombre

144

in the darkness, like a heaped fire gone out on the sea. Once the boat was out of the shelter of the land, the rain fell steadily upon it. The mast growled. The brown sail was out over the water and the rain poured off it into the sea. The sodden ropes, becoming taut, surrounded themselves with a mist of fine spray.

Out in the smoky channel the boat began to rise and fall, she shuddered from end to end as the waves exploded under her and the sea-wool boiled up on to the surface. The child, cold and wet, looked up in apprehension at his grandmother. She was heedless of the storm, she stared straight in front of her, her eyes hard and white and overlaid with an impenetrable glaze like mirrors. She muttered endlessly to herself. Her bonnet hung by its ribbon around her neck and her stiff disordered hair was being plastered down on to her head by the rain.

The people looked at one another in fear. They no longer tried to shield themselves from the pelting rain and their sodden clothes shone like black silk. They were silent. Some covered their faces with their wet hands. The dogs shivered and whimpered and were not reproved. Suddenly the boat banked steeply on its side as though it would turn over, and the sea smoked over it. Several voices cried out in terror. Rhodri's grandmother stopped muttering and looked about her. She left her seat. She knelt down in the water at the bottom of the boat and began a wild prayer. The boatman cursed her and pointed through the rain to the sea-plastered crags of the island. The child trembled with misery and fear. The woman sitting on the other side of him lifted her cloak and put it over him, covering his head. There, in the utter darkness, he could smell the sweat and camphor of her hard body. He could hear the quarrel above the storm, his grannie's voice screaming and the boatman shouting in reply. The boat plunged and shuddered and from time to time he heard a blow fall upon the taut cloak in a splashing thud as a wave came over the side. He drowsed. He could not remember landing. The next morning he woke up in his grannie's house.

*   *   *

A dog was yelling in unremitted agony. The child opened his eyes and heard some creature scampering rat-like across the hot roof sloping close above his head. Instantly he remembered and looked about in confusion. The grimy whitewashed bedroom was bare but filled up with sunlight. The window was a latched square of cobwebbed glass. He thought with a heavy heart of the meeting with his grandmother and the terrible crossing of the water. Hurriedly he got up from bed and looked out of the window. His eyes were on a level with a large vegetable garden where everything was green and glittering like tin in the sun. The dog was not to be seen but the cries continued in a high-pitched voice, the creature yelled hysterically and then sank into a series of agonised whimperings. The child, in deep distress, went down into the kitchen.

There it was dim and stifling, because a large piece of brown paper had been pinned over the window to keep the sun off the fire. He could not see his grannie. The room was bare but a great chained kettle hung boiling over the fire. His clothes were drying on a chair-back. He opened the kitchen door and looked out into the yard. The crying at once redoubled in intensity and he heard a drumming noise and the sound of a chain being rattled. The yard was a square of soft mud and dung with decaying outhouses surrounding it. In one corner was a barrow-load of dung overgrown with shoots of new grass. Near the kitchen door a great heap of his grannie's twigs leaned against a broken fragment of brickwork. He dressed.

It was an agony like a tearing of the flesh to hear the crying mount up again to a fresh climax of howls and yells. Soon it was plain the clamour came from an old outhouse on the far side of the yard, a broken-backed pig-sty with a roof under heavy dock and feverfew. The door shook as it was thumped from the inside and the chain rattled.

An old man trudged into the yard at a stoop leading a hulking ginger horse. He was wearing corduroy trousers and a ragged black jacket. An old hat was pulled down over his eyes. The mare had been working in traces and her chains jingled as she placed her great hairy hooves down in the mud. The dog heard the jingling and his crying increased in anguish. The child closed his eyes, he felt utterly engulfed, quite overborne and annihilated.

When he looked again, the old man had begun to pile the mare's harness on the bank. The child could see the sweat dark on her naked coat the same shape as the harness. The old man gave no sign that he heard the dog. Slowly he leaned one hand against the mare's flank and with the other began to milk her. As he plucked beneath her a rigid stream of warm milk fell with a splashing sound upon the mud. The child felt a deep stirring of his bowels. The anguish of the dog's crying was unheard as the white milk flowed over the mud and dung of the yard. In a moment the old man gave up and crossed to unbolt the stable. His movements had the clumsy ungainliness of an aged animal. The door of the pig-sty rattled under its battering as he trudged past, but he did not turn his head.

Out of the stable a beautiful golden foal bounded into the sunlight. The child's eyes opened with wonder and delight at the sight of her. She was the most beautiful thing he had ever seen and she was alive, she was moving and sunlit, and in his presence. Her coat was a pale limpid golden, a flamy honey-colour that seemed to flash off its fluid brilliance into the sunlight as she moved. Her mane and tail were already long and plentiful, to him they were as white as snow, but her muzzle had the dull smoky look of dark velvet. Her coming was a gap of ecstasy and pure silence. She trotted uncertainly into the middle of the yard, shying and prancing on her beautiful long legs, bewildered by the unsheltered brightness of the world. Then with a whinny she made for the great mare standing motionless and indifferent beside the bank and began to take suck. The child stared in blissful fascination. The marvel of the golden foal filled his heart, his delight ran through him like some great shaking draughts of ecstasy. Everything around him, while he gazed, fell under a spell of unassailable silence.

The old man, long-armed and high-shouldered, turned his back on the horses. Some cinders had been thrown down on the mud to form a path and he advanced over them with a stiff tread towards the house. His hoarse breath came with difficulty. He walked head down with a great hump-backed stoop, so that he was almost at the doorstep before he saw the child. Slowly he raised his eyes and Rhodri felt a sharp stab of anguish at the sight of them. They were dark as jet but the long lashes surrounding them were almost white, they were very thick and long, as dense as the hair of an animal, like a fringe of long yellow fur surrounding the edges of the dark lids. The face was rugged and bony, but the mouth hung open, the thick flesh of the lips seemed too slack and shapeless to cover up the hideous teeth. The old man said nothing, he stood and blinked at the child in morose suspicion, his great bony shoulders rising and falling as he gulped breath hoarsely through his wet mouth. Because of his stoop, the shining collar of his coat went out in a wide loop behind his neck and the sun shone on it in a half circle. He took off his hat and placed it on the sill. His long brown teeth showed and the broad back of his nose became loaded with a mass of wrinkles as he frowned into the dazzling sunlight. The child noticed the top of his head was hairless and not brown like his face, the dark skin ended abruptly where his hat had been and the pale scalp was thickly covered with beads of sweat. He lifted up his large bony hands and placed them with a clumsy action like a cap on the crown of his head. He held them there for a moment gasping for breath. Then he moved them slowly down over his soaking skin. The drench of sweat was squeezed forward along his scalp, it ran off his head before his hands and poured down over his face.

The child stared at him with the silent regard of complete fascination. Clogs clattered across the kitchen flags behind him and he could see his grandmother in the dimness beckoning with sud-gloved hands. Her stiff hair was wild and her eyes in that gloom seemed to have become completely sightless and transparent. The child went in towards her with fear. Behind him the explosive yelling of the dog broke out with unabated frenzy.

Soon the old man followed, bringing mud and dung into the kitchen. He sat down as though with exhaustion at the table. When he had replaced his sweat-sodden hat he began to eat in stolid silence. His hands were large and stiff, like great rigid claws falling upon his food. The child, seated opposite him, tried to eat his own breakfast, but he could not. He was in fear, his soul filled with utter confusion and bewilderment. He saw the old man breathing heavily and turning his food round in his slack mouth ; he saw the beautiful foal springing golden into the sunlit yard ; and he heard the incessant yelling of the chained-up dog. He began to pray in silence that the agony might be remitted.

"Mamgu," he said at last, looking round at his grandmother, "Mamgu, why is the dog crying all the time ?"

She came towards him with a look of puzzlement in her eyes. "Crying ?" she repeated, and turned to face the old man. She mumbled something which the child failed to catch. The old man shook his head slowly and resumed his chewing. The dog howled throughout the meal, and the chain rattled with agonizing repetition.

When he had finished, the old man got up and went out without speaking, a brown scum thick around his mouth. Rhodri said, "Mamgu, is he my grandfather ?"

She looked at him again in wide-eyed puzzlement. Then she nodded her head.

*   *   *

The child's cave, although it overlooked the sea, was not one of rock. It was a hollow under a grove of elders and, wearing only his ragged trousers, he sat at the mouth of it looking out over the water. The dog lay down panting at his feet and the golden pony, swishing her tail, cropped the green turf of the slope. The afternoon was still and silent, every leaf and blade of grass stood out brilliant and petrified in the intense heat. On an unsheltered rock cropping out of the turf the sun had kindled its uncoloured bonfire. The blue of the sky was flawless, it stretched out tranquil and unsoiled to the horizon and there was not a white cloud in it to cast the stain of a shadow upon the sea. From time to time, as the child watched, the breeze beat the water gently with ferns. At the foot of the slope, where the hill went into the sea in dark crags, the snowy gulls floated, they heaved gently upon a sea-swell that washed the black rocks in the milk of an endless caressing. The child

149

had been bathing ; before the tide was full he had ridden the golden pony naked along the lonely beach, splashing in the shallows of the sea.

The child came to his cave for safety and solitude. Every day now he was with the beautiful pony. At first he would stand by her when she was having suck and when she had finished she would come to him with milk on her mouth, blinking the dark globes of her eyes, black and lustrous. He was a little timid of her but she was gentle and gay and he soon learned not to fear her. He would put out his hand and stroke the soft sooty plush of her unquiet muzzle. When she had been weaned and placed in a field by herself, he used to go to the gate, before school and after, to speak to her. Directly she saw him she would throw up her head, point out her rigid ears and trot towards him with breeze-borne mane and outfloating tail. It was bliss to see her move rapidly over the grass with the grace of a great golden bird and the radiance of sunlight. She became more beautiful. Soon all the rough tufts of foal-fur had disappeared even from her long slender legs. Her white mane thickened, her creamy tail almost reached the ground. Her coat assumed a polish like brushed and smoothed silk, it was a golden orange colour, but in some lights paler, almost honey yellow, or caramel, and then sometimes again the rich bronzy lustre of old gold.

Often when he came to the gate she was waiting for him, standing with her glowing flank against the bars. Then he would speak gently to her and give her sugar or an apple, and sit astride her back. Round and round the field they went, she placing down the pure white horn of her unshod hooves delicately upon the grass and tossing her dense and snowy mane off her neck at every step ; he speaking gently to her her own praises, bending forwards to pat her neck with his hand beneath her mane. Her beauty and gentleness filled his imagination day and night. He loved the brown-eyed spaniel, but the mare was like a great flame of delight flaring up in the centre of his being. In his cave he crossed seas with her, climbed mountains, rode triumphantly through fallen cities. She accompanied him everywhere on the island. She dispelled the hauntings of the eyes, the animal stare of his long-lashed grandfather and the insane and transparent eyes of his grandmother.

One night the child had climbed out of his bedroom window into the moonlit garden. He found the dog, a little black spaniel, on a short chain in the ruined pig-sty crying pitifully to himself. The whole floor was under an oozing mass of pigs' dung. He held the dog against his body to comfort him and the little creature leaned up against him, shivering and whimpering softly. His nose on the boy's cheek was cold and moist, like the touch of a snail. In a few moments he began gently to lick the child's face with his rough tongue. Every time Rhodri moved, the dog seemed to cling to him and his crying began again, but now it was only soft and plaintive. The child unfastened the chain and took the dog into his bedroom. They both slept. The next morning he tossed the chain into the nettles. Later he raked out all the stale dung off the floor of the pigsty, and was sick. His grannie came and watched him at work, she stood at the door of the kitchen, her great flat eyes fixed immovably upon him, but she said nothing.

Rhodri's grandfather spoke seldom and never to him. The island was rocky and he laboured in silence. Once on the little beach below the farm the child sat down and began building a model in sand. It was large and elaborate, part temple, part fortress, part palace, with courts, arches, and towers, all ornamented with cockle-shells and glittering chips of glass-like quartz. The weather was sunny and he worked for several hours with the spaniel panting beside him. He had built it beyond the reach of the tide, so that he could return to it. At last, when he looked up, he could see the sun was lying down close to the water, its great red eye glaring across the flat sands, and he knew he would not be able to complete his work until the next day. As he moved back to admire the square-built walls, and the pebble-studded windows, he saw his grandfather driving the cart across the sands. The hulking mare was in the shafts and she came out of the sunset at a smart trot. The old man was standing up stooping, his hat over his eyes, but Rhodri could feel he was looking at him. The great horse approached at a good pace, her hooves clacking and her harness jingling. His grandfather drove straight on towards him. The mare went heedless over the sand-building and kicked it to pieces. The child sat down and hung his head. His grandfather had not turned to look after him. The cart rolled on. The spaniel, seeing the child with his head bowed in misery, came up and began to lick his face, in his eagerness to bring comfort he destroyed all that was left of the model.

The child's cave faced the sea. It was on the steep and barren side of the island where no one lived. He spent much of his time near it because the boys who persecuted him would never pursue him to this distance. To the cave he came to escape from his sense of solitariness and his unceasing desire to escape from the cruelty of the island. Here he forgot his fear of the brutal schoolmaster, and of the boys who hated him ; here he was not haunted by the watchfulness of his grandfather and his grandmother's muttering and her screaming in the night. It was to the cave he came to eat the fruits he found on the island, the bilberries and the little wild strawberries and once or twice when he had fallen into the sea he had lit a fire there to dry his clothes. But he would not light a fire in it now. A robin had built a nest in the overhead boughs and her little brood had already hatched.

From time to time a swallow cut over the grass, capering around the heels of the grazing pony. The pony's coat was honey-yellow, and where the light fell upon her back it shone like a saddle of pure silver. She had been rolling and upon her shoulder was a pale grass-stain, like a green patch of the most delicate verdigris. With her head drooped forward on her arched-out neck, a thick lock of mane hung between her ears on to her brow the colour of the froth of meadowsweet. Her muzzle had a dusty look as though it had been thrust into dark pollen. Her wavy tail broadened out and then tapered irregularly to a point that almost touched the grass. The boy did everything for her now. One day he would ride her through the world and everyone would recognize her beauty. The crowds in the streets would see him astride her with his legs along her golden flanks and as she trotted by they would acclaim the fluttering of her mane, and the elegant alighting of her ivory hooves, and the soft swansdown floating of her tail. She had begun to cast her glow and enchantment upon everything that existed with her in his imagination, and objects and sensations were recreated for him in her image. When he opened his eyes in his bedroom, the morning was a great horse, green and naked, ravaging the world outside his window. Watching the snow alighting gracefully, flake by flake, curving in the wind towards him over the hedge, he saw the beautiful stepping of white ceremonial hooves, advancing with delicacy out of the weather. And each day he saw in her more clearly the symbol of his escape.

In the evening the weather became chilly. A gull, perching on a rock near by, recalled him with the screeches of the splayed nib of her beak. Inside the cave the little robins opened their beaks as he paid them his final visit. He watched the pony gracefully curving her front leg forward on the slope and rubbing her muzzle against the inside of it. He whistled and her head came up and her ears stood erect. Then he made for the house with the dog and the golden pony following him.

*   *   *

After school the child went to look at the nest. He had known of it from the beginning, when it was merely twigs and a bowl of smooth mud, like a large acorn-cup. He had seen the six warm-hued eggs laid in it and he had visited the young ones almost every day to watch them grow. Soon they would be fledged. On the way he noticed that three of the boys who persecuted him were coming at a distance behind him. The boys had one day chased the golden pony to annoy him by making her sweat. They cornered her in the field and as she broke out one of them ran behind her clutching at her tail. She cast up her hooves and at one kick the boy's arm snapped like a candle. Since then they had attacked him constantly.

To throw the boys off his track he hurried down the path leading towards the bay. In a little he glanced behind again and he found he was no longer being followed, so he turned up the cliff in the direction of the cave. He wondered if the little robins would have learnt to fly. They completely filled up the nest now, they seemed to repose quite motionless on top of one another, forming a dome of smoky-coloured fluff enriched with a gleam of jewel-like eyes and with six yellow mouths that opened wide whenever he approached.

Rhodri stooped and went into the cave. He looked into the recess between the boughs where the birds were. He found only a heap of twigs with moss and horsehair hanging from it. His heart went cold, he felt an iciness lipping over into every part of his body. He dropped to his knees and saw the robins lying dead on the floor. Some had their heads cut off and others had been squashed with heavy stones. He groped his way out of the cave bewildered with rage and anguish. Standing on the path were the three boys who had followed him. They were stolid and old in their long, frayed trousers, their heavy faces dull and expressionless. One of them came up to him and gripped the front of his jacket. "Robbing nests," he said.

Rhodri tried to get away. He was afraid of the boys. They were bigger than he was, they worked on the land after school and were strong. The boy held him firmly by the coat, his face thrust close, heavy and repulsive. "Let me go," said Rhodri. "I didn't rob the nest. It was my nest. It was you who robbed it. I know you robbed it."

One of the boys came on to the path and spat on Rhodri's coat. Then he laughed. The child's heart thumped as though it had increased many times its normal size. He tried to wrench off the hand that was holding him, but the boy pushed him over backwards and bore him to the ground and lay heavily upon him.

At the pain of the fall the fear of his tormentors seemed to leave him and his flesh was possessed by an overwhelming frenzy of hatred. He writhed and struggled in the dust, trying to bite. He heard coming out of his own throat the scream of his demented hate, in its mastery he thought only of destroying the iron weight and the smell of the boy astride him. He lashed out savagely with his feet, he wanted to claw at the dull expressionless eyes, to smash into a pulp the bones and flesh of the stupid face. But he could not wrench his hands free, his wrists were held to the ground as firmly as with shackles. And gradually to his dismay he felt the great wave of lust and power ebbing from him. The knowledge that he had been impotent, even when nourished with this unaccustomed strength and ferocity, filled him with humiliation. He began to gasp for breath although all the time his lungs seemed full and bursting. He heaved his body up again convulsively and tried to squirm out from under the powerful unbudging body, but the passion had deserted him. Tears of dismay and frustration burned in his eyes. His body became limp. When he was quite still and the tears were running freely, the boy astride him leaned forward and struck him in the face. "You pig," he said, and slowly the immovable body was lifted.

Then the two other boys who had watched the struggle in silence and indifference came closer. One of them said, "He's mad, like his grannie." The other kicked the dust near Rhodri's head so that it fell over his face. The three then went away.

Rhodri crouched on the ground. His wrists burned like fire where he had been held down and he felt limp and weak, as though with long hunger. He made no attempt to rise. He sobbed bitterly on the path until his throat ached like a wound. No one came near. Presently a chill wind began to blow. He shivered. He had sweated during the struggle and now his bruised flesh seemed turning to ice. He felt sick and giddy. He crawled back along the path to the door of the cave and sat down in utter wretchedness, his face in his hands. His head throbbed. He would leave the island. He had no money but he would swim across to the mainland at low water and the golden pony should go with him. He wiped his face, and made his way back to the farm. His determination to escape filled his mind and his misery was overborne by it. Near the house he passed his grannie collecting sticks in her apron. She glanced at him from her staring eyes but did not stop or speak. He hurried on. The house was wide open and empty. He went upstairs and lay down on the bed, waiting for the darkness.

*   *   *

At midnight the child came down the beach with the pony behind him. In the distance, beyond the sea, was the dark mainland with a few lights sprinkled on the backs of the hills.

A full moon glowed rosy in the sky as though an unseen fire were lit against her curve. The tide was like black glass. It had gone out a long way and as the child went over the wet sand the moon was fragmentary in the little water-filled grooves and depressions of the beach, rapidly its light splintered into bright fragments and as rapidly flashed together again into one shining disc as the brilliant image was momentarily whole in a wide pool.

The child stood at the edge of the sea, wearing only his shirt and trousers. The night was calm and silent and very warm. The water in the straits lay motionless before him except for a strip of tide near the mainland where the current was running out strongly. Down the shelving sand into the sea he waded and the pony came after him. The water rose over his bare feet, over his knees, over his loins. In spite of the mildness of the night the sea was cold. When he was over his shoulders, he heard the pony snort behind him and begin to swim. She came alongside with only her head out of the water. Her mane floated and her nostrils were wide, shaped out like the mouths of trumpets. The boy flung his arm over her back as she passed him and kicked out. Together they went along, swimming side by side through the silent water. The child's heart was filled with unutterable joy. He was no longer fearful. He was escaping and the golden pony would be with him, she was bearing him away in the moonlight for ever from the island. Before long they would touch together the sands of the mainland. Many times he had swum in this sea but never so tirelessly and with such elation as now. The moon gave them ample light. His arm lay in an easy grip over the back of the pony, her white mane floated and the water swished up against her body as she kicked out with her hooves. Calmly, in perfect unison, they approached the middle of the straits.

There the current became stronger, soon the child could feel it beginning to wash his body away from the flank of the pony. She too felt the strain and although her pace did not slacken her breathing became heavier. Presently he had to clutch fiercely at her neck and mane to prevent himself being swept away, and he feared this might bring her head under. The sea was no longer silent, it began to rush with the roar of a great river, deep ridges appeared along the current as though the water were being miraculously ploughed. His body was dandled about from wave to wave. He thought that if he could get to the other side of the pony then the current would drive him against her flank and not away from her as it was doing at present. They had drifted a long way below the nearest point to the island, the outward-jutting rock on which he had hoped to land, and the force of the current showed no sign of diminishing. And in spite of the powerful swimming of the pony they did not seem to be getting any nearer the land ; instead they were being swept along parallel to it. The child feared that in this swift and rough water they would soon become separated. He determined to risk diving under the pony's head so that he could rest against her other flank. He was beginning to tire, but there all his energy could be used in swimming forward, not in holding on to the pony.

He drew himself up close to her, his arms around her neck. She went on swimming bravely, her wide-eyed head rising and falling as she went across the current. He whispered her praises and then dived. He tried with the ends of his fingers to maintain contact with her coat under water, but his hands were numb with cold and directly his head was submerged she was swept out of his reach. When he came to the surface she was nowhere to be seen.

The glaring of the moon troubled him and the splashing of the moonlit torrent in his eyes. He found himself moving along faster than ever. The gutter-like current lifted him on to the crest of a ridge and he glanced rapidly over his shoulders. The pony was behind him. She was still swimming strongly in the direction of the land but she did not seem to have made any headway. She seemed rather to be further out from the rocks than when they had become separated. The child realized that when he had dived he had not gone beneath her head at all. The current had hurled him forward and now its force was separating them more widely every minute.

He tried hard to swim parallel to the pony's head but he made no progress, the powerful rush of the broken water bore him along past the land. Soon he would be swept out to sea. He struggled afresh, but he was cold and nearing exhaustion.

His lungs seemed to be inflated all the time, and hard. His head went under constantly and the water roared in his ears. Each time he came to the surface the moon appeared to be held right against his eyes, dazzling bright and yellow as candle-flame. He spun round like a leaf on a cobweb. Rising suddenly out of the water, he glanced rapidly around again. In that hurried glimpse he saw the golden pony rising out of the sea ; somehow she had reached the land and was slowly making her way up the beach, shining like silver in the moonlight. The golden pony was safe. What would she do alone on the shore ? Would she wait for him ? He had to reach the land, he was bound now to get ground under his feet again, so that they could be together.

And then gradually he felt the current diminish. He had been swept round into a small bay, behind which stretched out a large dark fan of land. The tide seemed to have run out completely and the waters to have become slack. With what strength he had left he struck out in the direction of the land. He had not gone far when he found his arms touching the floating fronds of seaweed. His feet sank to the rocks. He staggered forward, falling and slipping among the underwater boulders. He found he was naked. In utter exhaustion and wretchedness he climbed over the rocks and reached a cut field bordering the sea. There he pulled a haycock over himself and took sleep into his body like a drink.

When he awoke the sun was shining brightly. The loud morning rang like strings with birdsong. His body ached. He could scarcely move. But the thought of the pony gave him no rest. He dragged himself out of the hay and stood upright. There in the distance lay the island floating lightly upon the varnished sea, calm and beautiful in the morning sun. Far out in the channel was the ferryboat, making for the island under her brown sail. And behind the boat was a small black object moving along at the same pace. The child recognized it at once. It was the head of the golden pony. They were swimming her back to the island.